Restoring Faith

Shaped by Love

By

USA *Today* Bestselling Author

MARION UECKERMANN

Contact Information: marion.ueckermann@gmail.com

Scripture taken from Holy Bible, New International Version®, NIV® Copyright ©1973, 1978, 1984, 2011 by Biblica, Inc.® Used by permission. All rights reserved worldwide.

Cover Art by Marion Ueckermann: www.marionueckermann.net

Edited by Paula Grundy:
https://paulaproofreader.wixsite.com/home

Cover Image Woman ID 61540443 Depositphotos © Subbotina
Cover Image Mountains ID 2034270 Depositphotos © Photocreo
Cover Image Columbine ID 22924090 Depositphotos © Vilor

ISBN-13: 978-1721965953
ISBN-10: 1721965955

PRAISE FOR *Restoring Faith*

The new novel by Marion Ueckermann, *Restoring Faith*, helped to restore my own faith by reminding me of God's ever-present grace and mercy. The characters in this true-to-life book are flawed and multifaceted, just like real people. Their doubts and fears, poor choices, and miscommunications spiral the couple down, down, down, until the reader is left wondering as to how they will ever climb into the light again. Truly an engaging book that had me racing through to find out how their faith in God would turn things around. A great read.

> ~ Jan Elder, Author of A Semi-Sweet Summer

In *Restoring Faith*, Marion Ueckermann writes about "real" issues as the reader witnesses a sixteen-year-old marriage in crisis. Marion has bravely explored a topic you don't often read about—a marriage in trouble. The characters are realistic and likeable.

Marion Ueckermann writes Christian fiction at its best as the reader can identify with the characters who are not perfect, who face life issues and who ultimately lift their eyes to their Father.

A perfectly wonderful read.

> ~ Julia Wilson, Book Reviewer at Christian Bookaholic

This book is a great example of how easily a misunderstanding can grow into a major rift. But it also shows how things can be restored, and not always how we imagine. A book that grows on you, from me wanting to shout and scream at the characters, to rooting for them at the end.

> ~ Clare Revell, Author of *Turned*

This book does an excellent job of portraying the problems and poor choices that lead to miscommunication, temptation, and ultimately breaking up marriages. While I read *Restoring Faith*, I found myself wanting to step in, stop both Charles and Faith and counsel them to listen to that still, small voice that was trying to change them. These characters are so well developed and realistic that the story will definitely speak to many readers' hearts. Excellent themes of the importance of being honest and open with each other and of learning to forgive in the same way that each of us wants to be personally forgiven for our own sins and failures. I highly recommend this book!

~ Becky Smith

Restoring Faith is an inspiring romance of restoration after misunderstandings of love grown cold. Where will Charles and Faith turn to overcome temptations and find happiness? Through conversations with friends, both churched and unchurched, and some unexpected plot twists, Charles and Faith find forgiveness and honesty is the best policy to restore a failing marriage.

~ Renate Pennington

I found *Restoring Faith* very easy to become lost in because the plot had strong and relatable characters and a well-developed storyline. Even if the whole marriage-breakdown situation doesn't apply to everyone, there will be areas which a reader could identify with. Whether you're strongly spiritual or not, there will be no reason not to become fully absorbed in the marriage woes of Charles and Faith, and how they will end up. Another wonderful story!

~ Paula Grundy, Editor

Something changed in the life of the family of Faith and Charles. With this book we can understand how silences and misunderstanding cause breaks in friendship and marriage. It's useful to be patient and to speak and talk with people to explain what we think.

~ Marta Aldrighetti

I loved this well-crafted story with exceptional characters that shows that the success of a marriage needs to be open and honest, with forgiveness and God at the center.

This book is recommended for those that love Christian fiction with a strong inspirational message.

~ Linda Rainey

In *Restoring Faith*, this author has written a story that captures so well the reality of a marriage that is not perfect and a couple experiencing the hurts that come from trying to work through the problems. It is a beautiful story following the characters as they face these problems and realize that turning to God individually and with their relationship is their only hope. This is another inspirational story from this author that I definitely recommend.

~ Ann Lacy Ellison

Dear Reader

We all mess up.
We all sin.
We all fall short of God's glory.

It is my prayer that through the pages of this book
you will come to understand that through confession
comes restoration, forgiveness, unity.

Be blessed.

To my parents ~

You left the legacy of a long and happy marriage;
you kept the vow, "Till death us do part."

Be on your guard, and do not be unfaithful.

~ Malachi 2:16 (NIV)

CHAPTER ONE

Friday, June 27, 2003

WITH HER fingers holding tight to the remnant of what was earlier a lengthy piece of chalk, Faith Young drew a line on the greenboard. The chalk screeched across the hard surface with a grating sound, and a chorus of groans from the handful of summer-school students, taking extra math, rose behind her. She turned around and smiled.

"And that, class, is how you do a linear equation."

A book slammed closed, and Faith raised her gaze to the back of the small class. Without a word, she strolled between the desks, stopping at the farthest one.

Dark brown eyes stared back at her from the good-looking, eleventh grade student. Faibian Walker. He raked his fingers through his wavy, shoulder-length brown hair, the tips already sun-kissed from the arrival of summer. There was something so hauntingly familiar about this young man, but Faith couldn't put her finger on exactly what it was.

"Is there a problem, Faibian?"

When it came to math and Faibian, there was always a problem. Sometimes Faith wondered if numbers were his issue, or due to his home situation. A single mom raising him, no father figure to look up to, to guide him, to help him with his homework…

At least her son, Michael, had that. Not only a father who was always there for him, but one who excelled at numerics. And with a high school math teacher for his mom to boot, certainly a win-win for their thirteen-year-old. No disadvantages like Faibian Walker.

"I still don't get it. I'll never get it. I hate math!" Faibian's chair toppled over backward as he shoved to his feet. He grabbed his books and fled the classroom.

"Faibian, come back!" Faith called after him, but the troubled boy's footsteps could be heard pounding down the passageway.

She wished she could help him more. Frankly, she'd been rather surprised to see him sign up for her summer class, nevertheless disappointed that he hadn't really seemed to want to be there. Then again, what teenager wouldn't prefer to be on vacation, enjoying the outdoors, than spending an extra month at school…learning math?

Maybe in the new school year she'd schedule a meeting with his mother—see what could be done to help Faibian not fail math in his final year of high school. She could offer to tutor him over weekends or after school for free, or something like that.

She strode back to her desk and addressed the students. "Class dismissed. Have a good summer vacation everyone."

"Thank you, Mrs. Young. You too," the students chorused as they filed out of her classroom.

Faith gathered her teaching material and stuffed it into her briefcase, thankful these extra few weeks of teaching were over. Now to get home and prepare for her guests. Her oldest brother, Brody, and his family were arriving tomorrow afternoon for a short visit. She couldn't wait to see them.

At least with visitors in the house, Charles would be more affectionate toward her. Heaven forbid the world knew their marriage was in trouble.

The two-week family stay had come and gone in a flash. Faith's heart squeezed against her chest as she stood on her tiptoes, one arm stretched high in the air, waving, as her brother's SUV grew smaller. How she'd enjoyed having them visit. She would miss them dearly. If only they could visit more often, but an entire day's drive separated Cottonwood Falls, Kansas from her corner of neighboring Colorado.

The person she'd miss the most, though, was her fourteen-year-old niece. As would Michael. With only a year separating the cousins—Charity, the eldest by eleven months—the two were almost inseparable.

Almost.

Thirteen-year-old boys didn't do kitchens. So when she and Charity did, Michael headed outside with his basketball to shoot some hoops.

What a lovely young lady Charity had grown into, and while Brody and his wife were off for hours on end, armed with their canvases and easels to capture the beauty of the Rockies, she and her niece had bonded once again over cupcakes, aprons, and a hot oven.

"Enough with the waving now, Faith," her husband muttered as he swung around and headed toward the house.

"Daaad..." Michael shook his head. "That's so not necessary."

Charles paused. He turned, jutting out his chin. "Well, your mother is still waving like a crazy woman. Their car is long gone."

So was the pleasant man she'd lived with for the past two

weeks, it seemed. How thrilled Charles must be that he no longer needed to pretend they were still a happily married couple. Even though Faith hated the charade, she'd enjoyed her husband's touches of affection, made purely for the sake of her visiting family. Maybe they should've gone camping during Brody, Madison, and Charity's visit—stayed in one big communal tent. Perhaps that way she would've felt the warmth of her husband's embrace during the night too. Instead, once behind closed doors, physical touch ceased, and Charles took his usual place in their bed...on the edge of the mattress with his back toward her.

Michael lifted his bicycle from where he'd discarded it on the grass and hopped on. "I'll be at Jeremy's house." He took off up the road.

"Make sure you're home in time for dinner, son," Charles called after him.

Faith knew why Michael preferred to be at his best friend's house rather than home with his mother and father. The Hamilton house was his place of escape from what wasn't going on at home.

Love.

She followed Charles up the garden path, and inside her heart beat in time with the dragging of her feet. How did they get to this place of...nothingness?

Charles grabbed the latest Wilbur Smith book from where he'd left it earlier on the kitchen counter and headed to the deck outside. He sank into the cushioned two-seater, nicely positioned in the shade.

For now.

He flipped open the thick paperback to the bookmark holding the spot he'd last read. The pages blurred, and Charles squinted his eyes. With a huff, he removed his reading glasses from the top pocket of his plaid, button-up shirt then slid them onto his face.

Better.

He hated being over forty. So many things didn't work the way they used to when he was younger. Not that forty-two was old by any means. Nevertheless, he certainly was starting to feel the effects of the aging process. Perhaps that was the logical explanation to his waning marriage. Or was he going through the dreaded midlife crisis? If so, why hadn't he gone out and bought a sports car then? Or a Harley? That certainly would have been far more fun to deal with than this daily burden of feeling nothing for his wife, the woman he'd vowed, merely fifteen years ago, to love and cherish until death parted them. The woman he couldn't get enough of…until a few years ago.

What had changed between them? How had they drifted apart like this? Had it been the move from Loveland to Fort Collins that started eroding their marriage? Or Faith's inability to bear a sibling for Michael? Or his own pursuit of the dream job, the dream house, the dream car? Well, he had them all—maybe not quite the dream car, although his Lexus SUV wasn't a bad fit. Had a red sports car filled his garage, however, he'd definitely have ticked the box for possible midlife crisis. And he had the dream wife to go with all his accomplishments. Faith was beautiful, classy, and intelligent. So why did he feel so empty, so unsatisfied, so distant?

Did the fault lie with Faith? Raising Michael plus still teaching high school math wasn't easy on her, and many nights she just flopped into bed, ready only for sleep. Many of those nights he'd had to bury his yearning for her. Had he buried his ardor one time too many?

Charles raised his gaze and stared out into the large backyard, the summer lawn a lush green, the trees clothed in leaves a darker shade. Deep down he knew part of the reason for his disquiet. Not only had he drifted away from Faith—whether her fault or his, or both of theirs—he had lost his belief in God as well. But who

5

would've guessed? He put up such a good front, wore just the right masks to get by every Sunday morning. Or when family visited.

But did he fool his son?

Michael was growing older now. Wiser. And from his son's outburst earlier, he doubted it. Michael could obviously sense that things at home weren't as they should be, as they had been for most of his life.

Faith saw right through him quite some time ago, so he'd given up pretending. Though he loathed himself for what he was putting her through, he just couldn't seem to stop—the scathing remarks flew out before he could take them back, and intimacy between them had reduced to meeting his physical needs alone. He'd come to care little for her emotional need to be held, to be told that he loved her. Even during those times, he just couldn't conjure up the old feelings that had made him fall in love with her.

Maybe they'd merely gotten too used to each other—returned to the friends' zone that had set them on this life path together. Except, he wasn't even a good friend. And he was a worse husband. A provider? Yes. A good father? Yes. A husband and friend? Not by Faith's definition.

Not by his either.

And then, perhaps this was just what growing old was all about. That's all. Fading sight. Fading hair—at least the color, his temples streaked with silver. Fading love.

Charles pushed the thoughts aside. There were better things to dwell on. He focused on the small print, bringing the book a little closer to his face.

"I'm off to the store, honey."

Faith's voice drew him from the words before he could even get lost in them. Without the slightest glance over his shoulder, he mustered an "uh-huh."

"Anything you need?"

A red Harley?

"Nope," he said, his answer curt as had become his habit. He chewed on his bottom lip, staring ahead at the garden again, his breathing rising.

There was a pause before Faith's sandals slapped against the wooden decking. He knew that walk. She was mad. And he didn't blame her one bit.

Tears stung as Faith hurried toward her Subaru station wagon. She opened the driver's door and sank into the seat, slumping over the steering wheel. Her chest rose and fell as she struggled to contain her emotions. *Lord, how am I ever going to fix my marriage when I don't know what went wrong, when my husband seems content not to try?*

Silence filled the cabin.

Great, even God wasn't talking to her.

She needed to unload on someone or she'd go mad.

Faith turned the key in the ignition. She was about to put the car into reverse when she paused. Leaning over, she dug out her cell phone from her handbag discarded on the seat beside her.

"Becky..." Faith sucked in a breath to steady her voice.

"Hey girlfriend, what's wrong?"

She and Rebekah Roberts had been best friends since preschool. Becky knew Faith better than she probably knew herself.

"Are you free for coffee?" Faith asked.

"Name the place, and I'll see you in fifteen minutes."

"HuggaMug Café?"

Becky sighed. "Oh dear, this must be worse than I thought. Be there as soon as I can."

Faith cut the call and backed out of her driveway.

Ten minutes later, she arrived at the coffee shop at the same time as Becky. Her friend wrapped her in a hug before they entered and found a seat. Probably the last table available. The place was pumping. But then, it was midmorning on a Saturday during the summer holidays.

Faith placed their order: a tall caramel macchiato for Becky and a vanilla one for her.

The waitress had barely turned her back when Becky grasped Faith's hands across the table. "What's he done this time?"

What had he done? Nothing, really, as usual. Just the same old indifference.

Faith pulled back her hands and shrugged. "Why blame Charles? Maybe I'm just feeling a little fragile because my family left this morning."

"Because I know you, that's why. And I know this has nothing to do with your family visit coming to an end and everything to do with your husband returning to the same self-centered jerk he's turned out to be. I know the drill. We've had this same conversation more times than I care to remember."

"Aren't you being a little harsh? He's not like that, Becky." At least he wasn't until a few years ago when he'd started to change. Somewhere around when the big four-oh crept closer. "Do you think this is just a phase, a midlife crisis he's going through?"

"Maybe. But whatever it is, it's not pretty, and I hate him for putting you through this hell. I've a good mind to—"

Faith's hand shot out, clasping Becky's arm. "Don't. Please. You can't become involved. Charles would be mortified if he knew I confided in you." Not to mention furious.

Becky leaned back in her chair as their coffee was delivered to the table. Eying Faith, she flicked her long, strawberry-blond curls over her tanned shoulder. "You know what you need? You need to have an affair. Show him he's not the only fish in the sea."

Groan. She should have known Becky was the wrong person to

offer marital advice. Her friend had already shown three husbands they weren't the only fishes in the sea, and Faith feared fiancé number four would suffer the same fate. She loved her friend, dearly, but what was Faith, a believer, doing seeking advice on such important matters from a non-believer? She should confide in someone at church. But whom? There was nobody but her friend she trusted with her secrets. And at the end of the day, advice wasn't really what she sought. All she wanted was a caring ear to listen to her, someone she could unload on, and Becky fitted the bill perfectly.

"An affair? You are joking? This is me we're talking about, not you. Besides, look at how that worked out for you...the first, second, *and* third time."

Becky pouted. "It might not have saved my marriages—perhaps I wasn't even looking for them to be saved—but it certainly made me feel a whole lot better."

Faith shook her head. "We're different that way, Becky. I just couldn't. I made vows to Charles—I won't break them, no matter how much he hurts me, or how unloved he makes me feel. My beliefs won't allow it. Neither will my morals."

"Never say never, girlfriend." A smile curved Becky's coral-colored lips.

Faith stared at her for a moment before blurting out, "What shade of lipstick is that?" Better to change the subject fast lest she entertain Becky's notion in the slightest as a last desperate attempt to get her husband to sit up and smell the coffee.

Speaking of, hers was getting cold. She lifted her cup and took a long drink.

"Coral Crush." Without giving her the manufacturer's name, Becky continued, her eyes bright, "Hey, Jeremy is out of town next weekend—conference of some sort. Why don't you and I take in a movie? *Pirates of the Caribbean—The Curse of the Black Pearl* released two weeks ago. Looks like it'll be loads of fun. A good place to forget about the world for a few hours over a bucket of buttered popcorn."

"I'll think about it, let you know during the week. All right?"

"Don't take too long. The tickets are bound to sell out soon."

Maybe going to the movies with Becky was a good idea. She didn't have to have an affair to catch Charles's attention. Creating the illusion might do the trick. She had to do something to fight for her marriage. She was at her wits' end.

CHAPTER TWO

FAITH TWIRLED the dishtowel in her hands as she followed Charles outside to the car. He hurried to load his clubs into the back of his SUV. The idea of going to the movies with Becky had danced around in her mind the entire week. But in the end, she'd decided not to go. Trying to make Charles jealous by creating the false impression of there being someone else in her life did not sit well with her. And rightly so.

Of course, she could just tell him she'd like to go to the movies with Becky, but he didn't really care too much for her best friend—probably because Becky was too straightforward with him. She pulled no punches. So Faith tossed that idea too. Instead, she bought herself a black, lace negligee, arranged a sleepover for Michael at the Hamilton's house, and planned a romantic, candlelit dinner and evening at home with Charles. She would fight to regain his love with everything she had. Charles would be playing eighteen holes of golf with a buddy, so she had the entire afternoon to set everything up. Wouldn't he be surprised when he walked into the house later on? It had been some time since she'd had the courage to initiate romance with him for fear of being rebuffed.

Her cheeks flushed at the mental image of what she'd planned for tonight with her husband. Excitement fluttered in her stomach as she formulated a way to be proactive and improve their marriage.

"What time do you think you'll be home after your game?" she asked as Charles opened the driver's door.

He paused in the gap between the door and the car. "I didn't tell you? I won't be home until much, much later."

"Oh." Her heart plummeted at the news that Charles wouldn't be home for dinner. There went her well-laid plans, up in smoke. Actually, more like a bonfire.

"I have some…uh…business to discuss with Jackson, so we've planned to shower at the club after our game and have dinner there."

"Jackson?" Not that common a first name, they only knew one.

"Moore," Charles clarified.

"From church?" Of course the same person. Why had she even asked the question? "I didn't know he was a client of yours." Jackson and Charles were friends, yes, but business dealings…

"Don't you believe it's him I'm having dinner with? What? Do you think I'm meeting some woman?"

"I–I never said that, Charles. I'm just surprised that I didn't know you had business dealings with your friend."

Charles whipped his phone from his gray golf pants and held it toward her. "Here, call him if you don't trust me."

Faith frowned. What was going on with him? His insistence of innocence only made him appear guiltier. Was he? Was her husband having an affair? Is that why he always seemed so distant from her? Seemed to have fallen out of love with her?

She pushed the phone away. "I do trust you!" She pivoted on her heel then hurried inside before she burst out crying in front of him. As the front door shut behind her she heard the sound of

Charles's car backing up out of the driveway. At a speed. Great, she'd given him yet another reason to distance himself from her.

The walls of the empty house suddenly closed in on her and her breathing increased. If she wasn't careful, she'd hyperventilate right there in the hallway. Well, she certainly wasn't going to sit at home all night, alone. She reached for the home phone on the telephone table beside the front door, lifted the cradle, and punched in the familiar number.

"Becky, any chance we can still do movies together tonight?"

Becky's laugh filtered through the phone. "I had a feeling I might get this call. I've already bought us two tickets. Do you want me to collect you, or meet you there?"

"I'll meet you there." That way she could leave as soon as the film was over, be home before Charles got back.

Charles leaned forward to turn on the radio as he steered the Lexus down the road toward the country club. A little light classical music might take the edge off his nerves. He wasn't looking forward to being vulnerable, bearing his shortcomings, his failures, his fears to probably his closest friend.

Business... Right. If Faith only knew what his "business" was all about tonight. Would she approve, or, like him, freak out? He would definitely not approve if she discussed their marital problems with someone else.

Charles had hoped to use the time walking the eighteen holes to chat to Jackson. Unfortunately, his friend went and arranged a foursome, hence his quick thinking for them to do dinner afterward at the club. Alone. He informed Jackson that he had something important he needed to discuss with him, lest he invite Richard and Gary for dinner as well.

Charles and Jackson teamed up together, playing against

Richard and Gary. By the time they reached the eighteenth hole, one thing was clear—Charles had definitely not brought his A-game. Half his shots had curved and landed in the rough; the other half positioned themselves precariously inside bunkers.

His brow moist with perspiration, Charles stepped onto the tee box. Blowing out a breath, he balanced the tiny white ball on top of the tee before sliding the driver from his bag. He positioned his hands together on the shaft then wiggled his backside and jiggled his legs. Just one good ball, that's all he asked, to save some face.

The club connected with the ball, and the small white dot flew into the air. Charles filled his lungs as the golf ball sailed down the fairway and plopped onto the green. He let out an excited yell as he fist-pumped the air. "Yes! Yes!" The ball rolled along the green toward the flagpole, stopping just short of the hole.

"Great shot, buddy." Jackson raised his hand to give Charles a high five.

Charles reciprocated. At last he'd done something right in this game. Jackson, on the other hand had played so brilliantly, he might just have single-handedly won this game for them. It all came down to the other players' final round—they'd both played well too.

In the locker rooms, Richard and Gary continued to congratulate Jackson and Charles on their win. The well-wishes should have gone to his friend alone. He'd done nothing, besides that last hole, to help them win.

"Hey, we should go into town and celebrate with a couple of cold ones," Gary said.

Jackson shook his head. "I have plans with a friend tonight I can't break. Besides, you guys know I don't drink."

"And you, Charles?"

Charles declined Gary's offer. He chuckled and smacked Gary on the back. "Don't let that stop you gents from going out and drowning your sorrows."

Gary flicked him with the edge of his towel and headed for a shower.

When their opponents finally left, Charles and Jackson ventured into the dining room, clean and clothed in fresh attire. Charles wasn't sure what he would've done had their golfing partners decided to stay longer at the club. Fortunately they hadn't.

After they'd seated themselves and placed their orders, Jackson stared at Charles. "So, what's on your mind? Judging by your game today, it must be something big."

Elbows on the table, Charles wove his fingers together and rested his head against his hands. He closed his eyes and exhaled. Where did he start?

He sucked in a deep breath and looked up. "I think my marriage is over."

Jackson's eyes widened. "What? You and Faith are splitting? Never!"

Charles proceeded to unload his burden while Jackson listened intently.

"I don't know what to do. How to change things. How to change me."

Jackson cut off a piece of steak and forked it into his mouth. He chewed, seemingly deep in thought. Finally he swallowed the piece of meat. "If you're asking for my advice, marriage is very much like a game of golf. You can play it alone, but it's not half as much fun as when there are two of you committed to the game. As in golf, you'll have good days, and you'll have bad days. But if you and your partner work together, you'll both be winners in the end. Don't bow out of the game early—get back in there and play as if your life depended on it, because it literally does. I've seen too many divorced couples totally mess up their lives, when they could've probably turned it around if they'd been willing."

Jackson's intense blue gaze bored into Charles. "Can I ask you something deeply personal?"

More personal than what he'd just told Jackson? Charles had a feeling that if he said no, his friend would continue to ask his question anyway.

He nodded and Jackson continued, "You seem to have lost your first love for Faith. Have you lost that first love for your Creator as well? Because therein would lie the root to your marital problems, and I would suspect the latter came first, even though you might not have noticed."

Charles swallowed hard. Had Jackson made that deduction based on what he'd just told him, or hadn't he fooled his friend in the slightest with the mask he wore every Sunday?

Faith carried the big bucket of popcorn, while Becky carried their sodas. Their seats were in the middle of the cinema. Becky eased into the row first. Faith followed, praying the seat beside her would remain empty. She hated sitting next to strangers. Whenever they'd gone to the movies as a family, which was quite a few years ago, she would sit between Michael and Charles.

The movie had just started when a rustle turned Faith's attention to the empty spots beside her. Great, a father and his teenage son.

The man sat down. As he eased into his seat, his hand touched Faith's arm resting on the armrest that separated the seats. He turned to her, the flickers of light from the movie accentuated the five-o'clock shadow along his strong jawline, lighting up his face.

She caught her breath, her heart slamming into her ribs. *No, it can't be.*

His eyes widened, and he whispered. "Faith? Is it really you?"

The teen beside him leaned forward and raked his fingers through his hair. "Hello, Mrs. Walker. Um, sorry about the other day." Without waiting for her to respond, he slumped back into his chair, eyes fixed on the screen ahead.

Faith tried to steady her breathing. How had she not seen the similarity before? Over almost a decade, she had watched Grayson Fuller do the same action with his hair. Far too many times. But, that was a lifetime ago, and besides the smoldering, dark eyes and the hair action, Faibian Walker didn't look that much like his father, although still a very handsome young man. Just like his father had been. Still was.

"I–I can't believe it's you. After all this time. You look great!" Grayson's low voice drew her back to the present and the dilemma of having her high school sweetheart sitting right beside her, telling her how good she looked. She hadn't had that kind of affirmation from a man in a very long time. It felt really, really good.

Becky leaned forward, most likely to investigate the whispers going on between Faith and the moviegoer in the seat beside her. Her face lit up. "Grayson Fuller?" She leaned across Faith to give him an awkward hug. "What are you doing back in town?"

A sharp shush from the row behind them had Becky back in her seat with a shrug. She mouthed a "we'll talk later" to Grayson before dropping her five cents worth in Faith's ear. "Well now, there's a twist of fate for you." She wriggled into her seat with a satisfied smile and shoved a handful of popcorn into her mouth, turning her attention back to the big screen.

Grayson leaned closer to Faith, his aftershave wafting dangerously up her nostrils. A masculine mixture of forest scents reminding her of early morning walks in the wooded foothills of Dark Mountain. "How have you been?"

She nodded her head. "Good." Her heart pounded as she stared at the lips that had captured hers so many times in their youth. She snapped her attention back to the movie, willing it to be over. It continued for two and a half excruciating hours. Every minute she had struggled not to think about who was next to her, his upper arm brushing against hers every time he'd leaned closer to whisper in her ear.

She hadn't seen Grayson since that fateful day, just before she'd started her final year of varsity where she was working hard to earn a bachelor's degree in mathematics. He'd told her over a milkshake at their favorite café that he'd screwed up—"just once" he had pleaded in his defense. He'd had too much to drink one Friday night while out with his friends—a flimsy excuse—and had made a new girl in town pregnant.

How could she have forgiven such infidelity, such betrayal?

Faith had emptied her shake in his lap before rushing home to pack her bags. She returned to Denver the following morning, one week early, telling her parents she had extra studying to do before the new year started, and it was too difficult to do so at home.

They hadn't questioned her refusal to see Grayson when he'd come around later that day. The letters he'd sent her in the following weeks had been dumped in the trash can. Three times he'd driven to Denver to see her. She'd sent her roommate out every time to send him packing back to Fort Collins.

It had taken that entire year to heal her broken heart.

After obtaining her degree, Faith had taken a teaching post at Loveland High. It was in this quaint little town, a half hour drive from where she'd grown up, that she'd met Charles. A year later, they were married, and Grayson Fuller became a distant memory.

How many promises had she and Grayson whispered to each other to be together forever? Theirs was meant to be a never-ending love.

Just like hers and Charles's, and look how that was going.

Grayson. Where had he been all this time? And why was he back in Fort Collins now? This chance encounter couldn't have come at a worse time in her life.

Lead me not into temptation, Lord.

Finally the credits rolled on the screen. Faith glanced at the time on her wristwatch and shot to her feet. Charles would surely be home long ago. She hadn't anticipated such a lengthy film. She probably wouldn't have agreed to come if she'd known. If only she'd stuck to her original conviction of not going out with Becky tonight. She would have avoided Grayson's and her paths crossing. But now that they had met again, she felt her world turning upside down.

"You ladies want to go for a coffee? To catch up?" Grayson directed his question to Faith.

She shook her head. "I–I need to get home. I'm late." She glanced away to avoid the dark gaze that always managed to draw her in. Nothing had changed in that department. She stuck out her hand. "It was nice to see you again, Grayson."

And now if he'd just move out of the way, she could get past and flee to her car.

He stood his ground, clearly aware of the advantageous position he held.

"I'd love to have coffee with you some time," he said to Faith. "Just to catch up. It's been so long. Do you have a pen?"

Becky whipped one from her bag and handed it over. She could seriously kill her friend right now.

Grayson glanced around. He bent over and grabbed his empty popcorn container from the floor. He scribbled his name and number on the side and handed her the striped cardboard box. "Call me." With a wink and a smile, he turned and ushered his son out of the row.

Faith stood rooted to the spot, watching his muscular frame walk away from her, willing the distance to grow between them. He'd changed, filled out in the right ways...a lot. My, he looked

19

mighty fine.

"So, are you going to call?"

She whirled around to Becky. "Are you crazy? That would be asking for trouble."

"Why? What's wrong with a cup of coffee between two old friends?"

Faith shook her head and moved into the aisle, still clutching the empty popcorn container he'd scribbled on.

Inside her car, she stared at the number for longer than she should have. Then she flattened the cardboard and stuffed it inside the cubbyhole.

Back home, the house stood in darkness. It was past eleven. Had Charles not returned home yet? Surely his dinner with Jackson had ended at least an hour ago?

She opened the front door then closed it gently. A soft click sounded in the silence. As she stepped into the living room, a lamp turned on, softly illuminating the room. Charles sat in the armchair beside the source of light, elbow on the armrest, his chin resting on his knuckles.

"Where have you been?" he growled.

"I...uh...didn't want to be alone tonight. The house seemed so empty after you left, so I went to a movie."

"Alone?"

She shook her head. "With Becky."

"I wish you hadn't. You know how much I detest that woman."

"She's my friend." Faith balled her hands into fists, her fingernails digging into her palms.

Charles eyed her, his gaze narrowing. "And you come home at *this* time of night after a movie with *her*? I rest my case. She's a bad influence."

"I— It was a long film...over two and a half hours. I left as soon as it ended."

Charles rose from the chair. "Where's Michael?"

"He had a sleepover at Jeremy's house."

"How convenient." Sarcasm dripped from his voice. "Especially when you knew I had plans."

"But I didn't, Charles. You were only supposed to be playing golf this afternoon. I'd expected you to be home tonight. I had plans for—"

"I tried to call you. Several times."

"I told you, I was at a movie. My phone was on silent." Faith's tone strengthened. She would not allow him to intimidate her. She'd done nothing wrong. "I hurried to get home as soon as I could, so I didn't look at it, didn't see your calls."

"Whatever, Faith. I'm off to bed. I'm tired. Tired from waiting up for you, worrying."

Pfft. Worrying? Right... Irked maybe, but worried? She didn't believe him for a second.

Charles disappeared down the passage leaving Faith alone in the living room.

She turned off the lamp then strode to the kitchen. She filled a mug with milk and placed it inside the microwave. A hot chocolate would help her sleep. As she waited for the milk to heat, she pulled out her phone. Six missed calls during the past ninety minutes. All from Charles. So, *he* could go out, do as he wanted, but not her?

Her chest rose and fell with frustration. Anger.

I don't think so.

She opened a new contact on her phone, labelling it GF. Then she typed in the memorized number. It might be nice to find out what had been happening in Grayson's life over the past eighteen years. After all, they hadn't only been sweethearts—they'd been best friends too.

CHAPTER THREE

SETTING THE EMPTY PIPING BAG down on the kitchen counter, Faith's gaze roamed over the boxes of iced cupcakes, settling on Becky beside her. Armed with a frosting-filled bag too, Becky leaned her lithe, jean and T-shirt clad body forward. Her tongue peeked through pursed lips as she concentrated on getting the cupcake topping as perfect as Faith's. Faith was glad her friend came over to help. It had been almost two weeks since their movie night, but to be honest, that was her fault entirely. She'd been avoiding Becky, hoping that by the time they saw each other again, her friend would've forgotten that Grayson had given Faith his number and asked her to call him so they could "catch up over coffee." Becky hadn't mentioned his name yet today, so it seemed Faith's plan might just have been successful.

Faith pushed her thoughts of Grayson aside, as she'd done every day since that strange night at the movies. Resisting the urge to groan, she straightened, ironing out the kink in her back with careful sideway movements. "Thanks so much for being here, Becky…doing all of this. I would never have gotten through this mammoth task of decorating all these cupcakes in time without you."

"Sure you would have. You just wouldn't have slept." Becky flashed her a smile. "Besides, what are friends for? And I certainly am grateful for the opportunity to spend some time with you in your lovely home. Doesn't happen that often anymore."

Faith drew in a deep breath, then exhaled slowly. Her friend was right—between school during the week and Charles home on weekends, the only time they ever got to spend together in this house was during school holidays. Even then, Faith was hesitant to have Becky over lest Charles arrive home unexpectedly, as he sometimes did, even though infrequently. Instead, she arranged coffee dates at one of their many favorite coffee shops or visited at Becky's house.

Well, today she had an excuse should Charles decide to pop home. She was racing against a ticking clock—those cupcakes had to be delivered to Rolland Moore Park this afternoon—and she had needed the help. Help she wouldn't get from her family. Both Michael and Charles were allergic to the kitchen. Wild horses wouldn't have dragged her husband or son to her rescue, even though Michael had been very apologetic as he'd rushed out the door this morning to hide at Jeremy's house until the cupcake storm had passed—his words, not hers.

Finished with the blue frosting, Faith discarded the piping bag in the sink to wash later. She grabbed a clean bag and popped a new nozzle onto it. This one would produce tiny rose-shaped blobs on top of those small vanilla sponges. She filled the bag—bright yellow this time.

Before starting on the next masterpiece, she wiped her hands on the apron that protected the floral, halter dress she'd donned that morning, the weather promising a hot ninety-two. Tomorrow's forecast held the same in store, perfect for the Colorado Day celebrations when their state would turn 127 years old.

She lifted a cupcake from the cooled baking tray and set it down in front of her. Raising the piping bag just above the treat, as she'd done so many times over the past two days, she squeezed, and a perfect rose perched itself on top like a crown.

"Hurrah, only a dozen more to ice, and we're ready for tomorrow's celebrations. I'm just thankful I don't have to serve these at the church's stall—Cupcakes, Cookies, and a Whole Load of Charity. I'm really looking forward to having the time free instead to stroll through the open-air market in the park." Her job was to supply a few hundred cupcakes for the other ladies of the First Baptist Church Women's Committee to sell. And voila, mission accomplished.

She glanced up at the remaining tray of bare-faced cakes. *Well, almost.*

"Rather a mouthful that name." Becky set the iced treat down carefully in the shallow box and moved on to decorate the next one.

Faith laughed. "It is. Cecelia Brooks, the president of our ladies committee, is a woman of many, many words. But I do love the play on the C's for Colorado Day." She paused to stretch out her back once again. She dreaded to think what she'd be like after she turned forty next year—it's rumored to be downhill after that. "Besides, I'd rather have spent the past two days baking and icing, than to miss any of the merriment tomorrow. And on the plus side, I got to have fun with my best friend."

Faith set the cupcake, now iced with a bouquet of miniature roses, inside the open box, alongside the other completed ones before grabbing another. "Are you and Lee planning on being there?"

Becky nodded, and a lock of strawberry blond hair escaped from the messy bun she'd created on the top of her head soon after arriving. She tucked it behind her ear. "But only in the early evening, once he returns from work. We'll grab a bite to eat and spend the rest of the night listening to the bands playing. That is if I can tear him away from all those craft beer stalls."

Becky raised her gaze to meet Faith's. "And you? Is Charles planning to grace you and Michael with his presence, or are you going alone again this year?"

Were they? They'd always celebrated Colorado Day together as a family. There was even a time when they still lived in Loveland when Charles would take the day off so that they could drive into Estes Park to go hiking for the day, or camping if the celebrations fell on a weekend. The last two Colorado Day celebrations, she and Michael had done without him. Charles had been out of town, both times at chartered accountants' conferences down in Denver.

He hadn't told her of any upcoming conferences, so he'd surely be home this year. Last week, she'd plucked up the courage to ask him if he could take tomorrow afternoon off from work so that they could have a family picnic in the park. All Charles had said was "maybe." Nothing more since then. She would have to remind him again tonight so that she could make preparations tomorrow morning. *Please, Lord, let him say yes. Our family needs this time together.* The last thing she wanted was Michael celebrating with the Hamilton's while she was left to celebrate the day alone. If that happened, she might as well join the church ladies selling their sweet wares for the day. And she really didn't want to. If she never saw another cupcake for a year, it would be too soon.

When they'd each put the final touch of frosting on the last of their cupcakes, Faith turned to Becky. "Think you could help me drop these off at the park? The church ladies are already there to oversee the setting up of their tented stall and to beautify it. While my car can handle the number of boxes, I sure could do with an extra pair of hands to carry them to the stand."

"Of course I can. Had planned to anyway." Becky elbowed

Faith. "What do you say we stop off for a coffee afterward? It's been a while since we last did that."

Faith couldn't help smiling at that idea. "Yes. I certainly could do with a pick-me-up. Should we try the place that's recently opened near the university? It's on the way home, and I've heard good things about it. I can't remember the name, but I know where it is."

"Definitely! So glad you didn't suggest the HuggaMug Café."

Faith cocked her head. "Really? I thought you liked that place."

"Oh, I do. Very much. It's just...that's where you always suggest we meet when you're feeling low. I'm so glad that isn't the case today."

Faith giggled as she closed the last box for transporting, then whipped off her apron. She washed the used piping bags and opened them on the dish rack to dry. The kitchen wasn't too messy; she'd finish cleaning up when she got home later.

"I guess if we're going to go out in public, we'd better freshen up."

Their hair brushed, lipstick freshened, and perfume revived, they returned to the kitchen to begin the arduous task of transporting the fruits of the day's labor.

"Will all these little babies be safe in the park overnight?" Becky asked as they walked to Faith's car, carrying several boxes each.

"Everybody is setting up today—no time to do it all tomorrow morning with the celebrations starting at ten. There'll be security. And as far as I know, most stalls are tented, so they'll be safe from the elements."

Faith spread out her boxes in the back of the station wagon, then turned to take the ones from Becky.

"So, have you contacted Grayson yet?" Becky asked casually as Faith slid the top three from her pile.

Faith almost fumbled the stack.

She sucked in a breath and leaned into the car to place the boxes beside those already there, using the opportunity to compose herself. She shook her head and spoke into the trunk. "Not a good idea to do so."

Her head and her heart had been at war over this very matter since it had landed squarely in her lap. How she'd love to catch up with Grayson, but she was so afraid it could lead to old feelings resurfacing. And that she didn't need. Or want. Finally, she came to the conclusion that she was far too fragile emotionally to have coffee with an old flame—even for the sake of the friendship they'd once shared.

She took the remaining two boxes from Becky and set them down beside the others. "Let's hurry and grab the rest—two trips tops—and get out of here. Somewhere downtown there's a tall hot drink with my name on it. I seriously need to get off my feet for an hour or two and relax." And there was no better way to do that than with her best friend and a shot of caffeine.

When all the boxes were loaded in the back of the Subaru, Faith reached up and pulled the liftgate shut. "Do you mind following me in your car?" Again, the paranoia of Charles coming home to find Becky's car in the drive surfaced. "It'll be easier for you to go home from the café than coming all the way back here."

Who was she fooling with her flimsy excuse for driving in two cars? Certainly not Becky, her raised eyebrow telling Faith she knew exactly why Faith had suggested they drive separately.

At Rolland Moore Park, they quickly transferred Faith's cupcake contribution to the tables at the church's stall, thanks to the additional help of Thomas Brooks. Cecelia had quickly instructed her husband to assist them before rushing back to bark out orders to all and sundry like a yapping Maltese.

When Faith set the last box down, she grasped Becky's arm.

"Let's get out of here, fast, before she ropes us into doing something else as well."

Giggling, they ran back to their cars then hurriedly drove off in the direction of Colorado State University. A few minutes later, they found two open parking spaces right outside the café.

Faith stared at the signage as she stepped out of her car. "Screamin' Beans?" Hopefully the name had nothing to do with loud music, and everything to do with a cup of coffee that blew your mind.

She glanced at Becky strolling toward her and smiled. "You think it's safe to go inside?"

Becky shot a look at the building, then stomped her high heels against the pavement and let out a shriek, beaming. "Just my kind of place."

Inside, the décor was vastly different from the quaint little places they frequented. Very upscale and modern. Irish-inspired bluegrass music drifted to the metal beams in the high roof. Faith inhaled deeply, the aroma of freshly brewed coffee permeating the air. Delicious. With a long wood and metal table running down the length against the large windows and several similar four-seater tables, the place had a distinct classroom feel. Blackboards with the food menu written in chalk filled the walls behind the serving counters. Just *her* kind of place. Groups of young people dotted the low bar stools and benches in the same design.

Becky leaned closer and whispered, "Very nice. With so many students here during summer vacation, can you imagine how this place must be pumping when the university is open."

"I was just thinking the same thing." Faith couldn't stop her hips from swaying to the music. She needed to find a seat fast. Except, none of the chairs looked very comfortable. And she had so wanted to relax for an hour or two before heading home. Nice as this place was, maybe they should head over to HuggaMug—they had such comfy armchairs.

Her gaze was still darting around the place when a young man dressed in a knee-length, black apron over his black T-shirt and pants neared, two menus gripped in his hand. He smiled. "You ladies looking for something a little more comfortable?"

Had she been so obvious in her search?

"Come, follow me. We have some lovely booths just around the corner."

Corner? How had she not seen there was more to this place than first met the eye.

Faith and Becky followed him to one of three curved booths, hidden by a wall upon entering. Wonderful. Nice and private, and with padded seats.

"Thank you." Faith shimmied onto the cushioned bench.

Becky joined her on the other side of the table.

The waiter smiled. "My name is Daniel, and I'll be serving you today. I'll give you ladies a few minutes to check out the menu."

"Oh, that won't be necessary. We'll have two tall macchiatos—one caramel, one vanilla."

Another smile teased Daniel's mouth as if he knew something they didn't. "Have you been to Screamin' Beans before?"

Faith shook her head as Becky answered, "No."

"I'll give you a few minutes with that menu, then. Trust me, you won't be sorry." And with that, Daniel disappeared to clear a nearby table.

Faith opened her menu and scanned the contents. "Oh my, he wasn't kidding. How on earth are we going to choose?" Some of the offerings she hadn't even heard of.

Becky whipped open her menu, her big, blue eyes widening. "I see what you mean. Maybe we should just wait for Daniel to return and suggest something."

"Look at this one," Faith said. "An affogato—a scoop of vanilla gelato topped with a shot of hot espresso."

Becky licked her lips. "*And* you can have that with a shot of Amaretto as well, or a different liqueur."

"Um, I'll pass on the liqueur, but I seriously don't know what to drink. They all sound so delicious. I'm so spent after all that baking, however, that at this point I'd gladly eat the coffee out of a tin with a spoon."

"You ladies look confused. Need any help?"

Faith's heart bounced in her chest like a rubber ball. Her head shot up from the menu she'd buried it in. Grayson. She stared into his dark gaze, her mouth going dry as ground coffee beans.

CHAPTER FOUR

CHARLES MOVED his laptop's external mouse and pointed the tiny arrow on the screen at the save option. He left clicked, closed the spreadsheet, then shut the laptop's lid. He'd resume after the meeting with his financial team. But first, coffee. He had time to savor a cup at his desk before moving to the boardroom. He lifted the phone from the cradle and dialed his secretary's number.

"Yes, Charles," came her sweet voice.

"Juliette, would you mind making me a quick cup of coffee? And one for yourself. Then come into my office. Let's go over the agenda one final time before the meeting."

"Two coffees coming right up."

The line went dead, and Charles hung up. What would he do without his trusted secretary of nearly two years? Juliette was a stalwart assistant—the backbone of his office.

Hands behind his head, Charles leaned back in his chair and arched, curving the kinks from his spine. He should get out of this chair more often.

There was something else he should do...call his wife. He still hadn't given Faith an answer about tomorrow afternoon. If he was going to start putting in an effort to make his marriage work, to fall in love with Faith again, no better time to start than now. He just hoped it wouldn't be as arduous and unfulfilling a task as trying to return to his first love with God, as Jackson had suggested.

He'd mulled over Jackson's words for days after their dinner, and only earlier this week had he ventured to start reading his Bible again. He'd tried his hand at praying daily too. His prayers felt as if they boomeranged off the ceiling, and God's Word seemed as dull and dead as time spent with his wife. Was it too late for him and Faith? What about him and God?

He wouldn't know unless he tried. Unless he persevered. For a while at least, anyway. He was not a patient man, preferring to see instant results, and he feared his marriage and soul were already doomed before he could give either a chance for revival.

Charles lifted the phone again and dialed home. No answer. Strange, Faith had said she'd be up to her eyeballs in frosting all day long. He gave it a few seconds and tried once more, just in case Faith had gotten to the phone when he'd hung up. The ringing still went unanswered.

Maybe she'd popped out to the store, run out of frosting or something like that. He tried her cell phone. After buzzing in his ear, the call went to voicemail.

"Faith, it's Charles. Call me."

He pursed his lips and frowned as he hung up. This was so unlike her. He could always get in contact with her, even when she was out or driving.

"And that scowl?" Juliette strode into his office bearing two steaming mugs. She shut the door with her foot. "That way we won't be disturbed while we go through that agenda."

She set the mugs down on his desk and settled into a chair opposite Charles.

Not wishing to discuss his marital issues with his secretary,

Charles ignored her question and drew his mug closer to peer inside. "Are those tiny marshmallows floating on top?"

Juliette laughed. "Just trying to sweeten you up before this meeting. I know how rough they can get at times. I do take the minutes, remember. But it seems perhaps I should've put a few more in your coffee. What's up, boss, you don't look happy."

Charles shook his head. "It's nothing."

Juliette leaned forward, and Charles couldn't help noticing that one more button should have been fastened on that figure-hugging blouse of hers. He averted his gaze back to the contents of his mug.

Juliette touched his hand. "I want you to know that you can talk to me about anything, Charles—not just work." She lifted her mug and eased back into her chair, eyeing him over the porcelain rim as she took a sip. "I have been told on numerous occasions that I'm a good listener, and there's *nothing* I wouldn't do for you."

Charles swallowed hard and shifted in his seat. But his discomfort had nothing to do with his chair. Was Juliette intimating what he thought she was? Surely not?

He cleared his throat. "Thank you, Juliette. You're a faithful worker. I'll be sure to remember your offer when I need a friendly ear. But now we need to run through that agenda, finish this coffee, and get to that meeting."

Oh no, what was he doing there? Faith offered a wobbly smile. "Grayson!" Avoiding eye contact, she quickly looked away.

Like a cat who'd discovered an open bottle of fresh dairy cream and tipped it over, Becky's mouth curved. "This is a nice surprise. How good to see you again, Grayson. Won't you join us? Please." Oh yes, Becky was ready and willing to savor the mess she'd just willingly created.

Maybe Charles was right. Maybe her friend was trouble.

Grayson pushed away from where he'd leaned on the table to greet them. He straightened, and he seemed taller than she remembered. Maybe that was just because she was seated and he was standing, towering above them.

"I don't want to intrude. You ladies are obviously here on a girls' afternoon out. And believe me…" His brows raised as he nodded. "I know how important those are to women."

A knot twisted in Faith's stomach. Had he been with many women over the years? He must have…the way he'd said he knew how important time-outs for women were… So much for everlasting love. But she should have known better—if he couldn't be faithful to her when they were together, why on earth would he be chaste in the years following their breakup?

Had he ever married? Her gaze drifted to his left hand. It bore no telltale signs of a gold band, or of having recently worn one. In fact, his hands gave away nothing. Though they weren't like Charles's—soft and refined, the product of years behind a desk—they weren't the hands of a blue-collar worker either. Muscles rippled up his forearm, all the way to the short sleeves of the black T-shirt that spanned his broad chest.

What have you been up to all these years?

"No need to run off," Becky said. "We haven't seen you in a lifetime. We're dying to hear what you've been up to, and what brings you back to Fort Collins. You did leave, didn't you?"

"Oh yes, I left all right. Only came back to stay a couple of months ago." Grayson took a step toward Faith's side of the table. Great.

Faith shifted up on the curved bench to make space for him to sit. It was obvious he had no intention of going back to where he'd suddenly appeared from.

He sat down on the vacated spot and rubbed his large hands together. "So, if you're here for coffee, could I make some suggestions? I know the menu can be somewhat overwhelming the first time." His head oscillated between them. "This is your first time here?"

"Yes," Becky answered. "Seems you frequent this place, though."

Grayson smiled, the dimple Faith remembered so well forming on his right cheek, almost hidden by the stubble that framed his jaw and lips. "Something like that."

He slid Faith's menu out from under her hands and opened it. "On hot days like this, most women love to try an iced coffee. I love it too and highly recommend the blended iced cappuccino." He cupped the side of his mouth, directing his words to Faith and Becky. "Don't tell anyone, but the secret's in the chocolate milk. And the cream gives it that added richness."

Grayson's gaze bored into Faith's. "I remember well the sweet tooth you had."

Becky laughed. "Nothing's changed in that department for Faith."

"You'll really enjoy this. I promise," Grayson said, his voice low, the words once again meant for Faith alone.

"Sounds great! I'll have one of those." Becky slapped her menu closed and pushed it aside, no longer needed.

Grayson flashed Becky a smile before turning his attention back to Faith. "One for you as well?"

Faith nodded. "Why not? Although I'm certain if it's as decadent as it sounds, that chocolate and cream is going to go straight to my waist." She gave herself a mental slap. Why had she said that, directing Grayson's thoughts to her body?

A low chuckle rumbled from his chest before it spilled from his mouth and filled the booth. He'd always had such a hearty laugh. One of the reasons she'd loved him.

"Last time I looked, which was only a few nights ago, that

waistline looked mighty fine to me."

Heat crept up her neck and kindled her cheeks.

Grayson glanced around, then indicated with his fingers for Daniel to come closer. How did he know Daniel was their waiter?

"Three blended iced cappuccinos, please, Daniel."

The young waiter shot Grayson a smile. "Great choice! Your suggestion, Mr. Fuller?"

Grayson laughed and cocked his head. "I *do* know what's popular."

Daniel disappeared and the trio made small talk—mostly about the scorching weather—until he returned, balancing the three decadent iced-coffee treats on a tray. He slid the tray onto the table then placed the tall glasses in front of them, Becky first, then Faith. As he set Grayson's glass down, he gave a sheepish shrug. "You know how it goes…ladies first."

"Wouldn't expect anything else from you, Daniel. Oh, and no charge for this. I'll straighten you out with a service fee later."

Faith sucked the icy liquid through the straw. Grayson was right, this tasted divine. She eyed him, then swallowed. "No charge? What, are you the owner of this establishment or something?"

With a twinkle in his eye, he answered, "Something like that."

"Get out of here!" As usual, Becky's voice was larger than life, and Faith was grateful for the bit of soundproofing the booth offered. "So that's what you've been up to for the past eighteen years…building a coffee empire."

"Hardly. This is new territory for me," Grayson responded.

"You could have fooled me. This place is amazing." Becky lifted her glass, and wrapped those coral-colored lips around her straw.

Gripping his glass with one hand, Grayson relaxed back into the seat. He stretched out his free arm on the backrest of the bench that wrapped around the booth like a horseshoe. He lifted the iced coffee and took a long drink. As he leaned forward to return the glass to the table, his arm brushed against Faith's shoulder. A strange sense of déjà vu sent a shockwave through Faith, and she shifted a little farther up the bench, away from him. Away from the memories his touch invoked.

Grayson blew out a heavy breath. "I haven't always made the best choices in my life. I guess I was afraid of the responsibilities of fatherhood. I left Fort Collins shortly after Faibian was born."

"You never married?" Faith raised a questioning brow. "I–I only ask because your son has a different last name."

He shook his head. "No. That's why Faibian's mother registered him under her surname." He shifted in his seat and leaned forward, folding his arms on the table. His face grew somber. "I drifted from one city to another, one dead-end job to another. Finally, I found myself in The Land of Milk and Honey. It was there in sunny California that I started working as a barista in a coffee shop and learned my trade. Eventually I was working for one of the trendiest coffee shops on Rodeo Drive."

Becky leaned across the table and whispered, "And you made *that* much money as a barista, that you bought this place?"

Grayson laughed. "I wish. Actually, my father passed away last year. As I was his only living relative, my mom having died eight years ago, I inherited everything."

Faith reached for his arm, giving it a comforting touch. "I'm so sorry. I didn't know that either of your parents had passed on." She quickly retracted her hand. "Mine passed away too. A few years ago."

Her eyes roamed the room again. His father had been quite wealthy, so it figured he'd be able to afford to open a place like this.

"Are you staying in their old house?" Why had she asked that?

Stupid!

"No. That house was way too big for me. And Queen Anne is so not my style, either. I sold it as soon as I was able to—bought myself a three-bedroom, two-story garden condo. I like the communal living."

"Well, this coffee shop is simply amazing." Becky's mouth curved into a wide smile. "You've done well for yourself, Grayson."

"Your father's death brought you back to Fort Collins?" More questions? Seriously? She should sit back and sip her iced coffee and leave Becky to ask any questions before moving along home.

"Yes and no." Grayson twirled his glass around, seemingly in thought. He paused the twirling. "I'd been contemplating moving back shortly before my father suddenly died. Faibian needed a father figure in his life. His mother called me one day to say it was time I stepped up and had Faibian spend more than summer vacations with me. She said if I didn't want him to turn out to be a failure like myself, I needed to be a more permanent fixture in his life."

"You're no failure!" Becky swooshed her hand through the air. "All of this is proof of that. You sure showed her. Good for you."

Grayson shook his head again, chuckling. "I didn't do it to show Lucinda up; I did it because it's my passion. And I did it for my son—to be closer to him, and to leave him a legacy."

He remained silent for a while, his mouth drawn, pensive. "I'd wanted to mend fences with my father...we didn't part on good terms when I left town. But I left things too late, never managed to fix things with Dad. I never want that to happen between me and Faibian. I've come to realize that life is too short; opportunities can so easily pass us by if we don't grasp them with both hands while we can." He stared at Faith, and her face warmed.

"So true." Faith hurried to finish her drink. She glanced at

Becky. "I guess we should be going. Thanks for the coffee, Grayson. It was nice seeing you again."

Becky grasped Faith's arm as she started to rise, not that she could go anywhere. With both Becky and Grayson each occupying a seat at the ends of the wraparound bench, Faith was stuck. Thoughts of jumping right over the table sprang to mind, but she quickly dismissed them. If she'd been wearing Becky's jeans, then maybe. But in this dress...not going to happen.

"Whoa, girl! What happened to I want to relax for a few hours?" Becky asked.

"We've been away from home almost two hours already. I still have a kitchen to finish tidying before Charles gets home."

"Charles? Your husband?" Grayson shifted to the end of the bench and stood.

Forest scents tantalized Faith's senses once again as she shimmied past him.

Becky didn't budge. "I think I'll stay awhile longer. Maybe try a hot coffee."

Seriously? Did her friend have her eye on fiancé number five?

Jealousy stabbed...at least that's what it felt like. Ludicrous, couldn't be. And surely Becky wouldn't go after Grayson. She knew their history.

"Suit yourself," Faith said nonchalantly. "Catch you at the festivities tomorrow, perhaps?"

"I hope so." Becky shifted her attention to Grayson and gave him a warm smile. Too warm for Faith's liking. Was this a mistake, her leaving without Becky? Nothing she could do about that now.

"Grayson? You going to join me for another coffee? There's still so much I want to hear about you." Becky scooted back in the seat and patted the cushion beside her.

Grayson brushed his fingers through his short, wavy hair. Was he uncomfortable at the notion of sitting there alone with Becky? "I should probably get back to work. Can I walk you to your car, Faith? I need to ask you something."

"Um, sure. Okay." Faith stepped past Grayson then leaned over to give Becky a hug. "Behave yourself, now," she whispered.

Becky's soft giggle drifted over Faith's shoulder. "If I can't behave, I'll be careful. I promise."

Faith pursed her lips and cocked an eyebrow at her friend before turning to go. "My car is parked just on the other side of the street."

Grayson held the café door open for Faith to step outside. Hot air rushed at her as she left the air-conditioned environment behind.

He quickly fell into step beside Faith. Her heart pounded as they strode across the street. What did he want to ask her?

"You didn't call," he said as they neared her Subaru.

She shook her head. "I didn't see the purpose. Besides, it would be inappropriate. I'm married, and I've no idea if you are either."

"I'm not. Never have. And it was only supposed to be a get-together for two old friends to catch up. Nothing more."

Now she felt foolish. Had she really thought his suggestion was to worm his way back into her already complicated life?

"We've done the catching up now." She unlocked the car with her key fob and placed a hand on the door handle. "What did you want to ask me?"

"Faibian needs help with his schooling. While I can help him with some of his subjects, I was never great at math…despite all your efforts back in school to explain it to me."

Faith couldn't help smiling and shaking her head at the memory.

"Would you consider giving him private tutoring?" Grayson asked, his eyes pleading. "Doesn't matter what it costs."

"Funny you should mention tutoring. After Faibian stormed out of my final summer school class, I'd planned to contact his mother in the new school year to suggest exactly that." But that was before she knew who Faibian's father was. That information certainly changed things.

"You did? How about I give you a few days to think about it, and we meet here next week sometime to discuss a way to proceed?"

Faith drew in a deep breath. Would this decision lead to trouble, or help a young boy in trouble? She wouldn't know unless she tried. Besides, she'd managed to stay out of trouble her entire life, and she didn't plan to change things now.

She ventured a look into those dark pools. "How about next Thursday? Two o'clock?"

"Make it one, and you can have lunch with me. My treat."

CHAPTER FIVE

FAITH SAT in a recliner in the lounge, reading her Bible. Or rather, trying to read. Concentrating on the words was difficult as her thoughts continually drifted. Charles had actually agreed to take time off work today to go to the celebrations at Rolland Moore Park, albeit only from around three. Still, something was better than nothing. As soon as she was finished having her quiet time, she'd get ready then pack a picnic basket for their family of three.

"Mom, are you and dad getting a divorce?"

Faith's head shot up. Michael stood in front of her, sadness filling his soft blue eyes. He looked so much like his father, her heart ached.

Easing upright, Faith set her Bible down on the table beside her and reached for Michael. Grasping his hand, she pulled him closer. "Sweetheart, no! Why would you think such a thing?"

He shrugged, skewing his mouth down on one side. "I dunno. Things are just...different. You and Dad...you don't laugh together anymore. You don't even talk much. And I— I just want things to be the way they were."

"So do I, son. I know things have been a little rough around here lately, but you know what? I believe things are about to change." She gave him a glowing smile, adding some extra wattage to calm his fears. "I forgot to mention, your father's coming to the Colorado Day celebrations with us. We're going to have a picnic later this afternoon and listen to the bands, maybe have a dance or two. It'll be fun, you'll see."

Michael nodded, his eyes brightening. "I hope so."

He turned to go, then stopped. "Mom, I'm praying for you and Dad."

Faith's gaze blurred, and she dabbed the corners of her eyes with the tips of her fingers. "So am I, sweetie. So am I."

Michael thumbed over his shoulder to the front door. "Can I go and play at Jeremy's house until we leave?"

Faith's heart warmed to see excitement return to his demeanor. "Aren't the Hamiltons going to the celebrations?"

"I dunno. If they are, can I go with them? Meet you and Dad there?"

"Of course you can. I'll give Jeremy's mother a call and check with her. Otherwise, we'll pick you up at their house on our way. Should be a little before three thirty."

Michael rushed back to Faith and flung his arms around her. "Thanks, Mom. You're the best!"

If only Charles still thought that.

With a wave, Michael rushed out the front door, and Faith watched him disappear down their driveway on his bicycle. She sank back into her chair, closing her eyes.

Father God, thank you for this beautiful new day, and with it, new mercies from Your hand. Oh Jesus, bless this day with Your presence, surround me with Your love. Lord, I pray that You will revive Charles's love for me. And for You. Especially You, Lord, because when that is right, everything else in our marriage will fall

43

into place. Help him to love me, Jesus, as You love Your church.

Faith spent several minutes more in prayer, praying for the needs—physical and spiritual—of her family and friends: Brody, Madison, and Charity in Kansas, and her younger brother Tyler, and his wife, Hope, down in Florida—Clearwater, Tampa to be more precise. Hope had lost a baby early in the third trimester nearly eighteen months ago. Tyler didn't say much, but Faith was certain they were struggling with the loss.

And if Faith correctly read between the lines of her conversations with Charity during Faith's older brother's recent visit, life wasn't all that hunky-dory in the Kansas Peterson household either. Seemed their whole family was dealing with one issue or another.

After praying for her siblings and their families, Faith went on to offer up a prayer for Becky and for Grayson as well. She prayed for a strengthening of the ties between him and his son; she prayed for wisdom about tutoring Faibian.

Finally, she said amen and rose.

She made a phone call to Hazel Hamilton, confirming that they were going to the celebrations. Faith promised to contact Hazel once they were there.

Loathing the rush of last minute preparations, Faith strode into the kitchen. She should have enough options in the pantry and fridge to avoid a trip to the store. She placed the picnic basket on the kitchen counter and set about filling it with soda, potato chips, hot dogs, and half a dozen of the cupcakes she'd set aside. She cleared a shelf in the refrigerator and placed the basket on it. There were still a few hours before Charles would return home.

Faith couldn't shake the feeling that something was missing. But what? Her gaze flitted around the room. What more did they need besides food and drinks for a picnic?

A picnic! Of course. She hurried to the linen cupboard at the end of their lengthy passage and pulled out a plaid blanket in autumn shades. *Can't picnic properly without one of these.* After rolling the blanket tightly, she set it down on the kitchen counter.

With the picnic stuff taken care of, Faith returned to her bedroom. She applied her makeup, curled her hair with a curling iron, and then brushed out the long locks, reforming the curls between her fingers.

Standing in front of her closet, she mulled over her choice of clothing that morning. Eventually, she decided to change out of her blouse and jeans and put on a pretty, white cotton dress with cap sleeves. It was far too hot outside to be bothered with long pants, and she wanted to look soft and feminine for her husband. She complemented the outfit with dainty, low-heeled red sandals. A splash of color always worked well with white. And for some strange reason, men apparently loved red.

After a few sprays of her favorite perfume, Faith returned to the kitchen and poured herself a glass of iced tea. She carried the cold drink outside on the deck to enjoy in the glorious sunshine. Fortunately, the umbrella was still up and one of the couches just caught the shade. She sank into the protected spot and sipped the iced tea.

When the glass was empty, Faith glanced at the time on her wristwatch. Sigh, still three and a half hours to go. Perhaps she should take a drive to Rolland Moore Park, walk around for a while. Charles might not want to see the various stalls, and she'd lose out. She'd have at least two hours to stroll around before needing to leave to be back home before Charles.

Yes! That's exactly what she'd do to pass the time.

Faith gathered her handbag and car keys and headed for the front door.

Rolland Moore Park was alive with families celebrating the day. She strolled from one stall to the next, sampling food, feeling fabrics, trying on jewelry. Up ahead, a queue of people lined up in front of the church's stall. Hopefully her brightly colored cupcakes were the attraction.

She should find out how sales were doing.

Faith hurried over to the large white tent and opened the flap, popping her head inside the staff entrance.

Cecelia Brooks gasped as she spotted Faith and raised her eyes toward heaven. "Thank you, Lord. Faith Young, you are a sight for sore eyes, and heaven-sent if ever anyone was. Come on in quickly, girl, and give us a hand."

A hand? She'd already given the church several by supplying the tiny treats.

"Word of your delicious cupcakes has spread, and we can't keep up with the sales. On top of that, Judy Banks called in sick, so we're down one person." Cecelia shoved an apron at Faith. "Here, put this on."

"But—"

"No buts, Faith. The Lord needs your help at His cake table. Just for an hour or so. Please."

Faith hated hearing Cecelia beg. It was almost as bad as listening to her bark.

"All right, but I can't help for more than an hour." She glanced down at the giant embroidered cupcake on the front of the apron and groaned. As if she hadn't had her fill of making the small cakes yesterday. She was just thankful Becky would only be at the park later that afternoon so she wasn't likely to stop by. Her friend would never let her live this one down.

"Yes, yes," Cecelia nodded, pushing Faith toward the serving table where boxes of her cupcakes and other sweet wares were on display. Had Cecelia even heard a word she'd said?

Just before two p.m., Charles shut his laptop and slid it into its bag. He smiled at his idea to get home a little earlier and surprise Faith. It had been so long since he'd done something nice for his wife that a flutter of excitement nestled itself in one corner of his stomach. Was this progress? A step in the right direction to get his marriage back on track, to regain his first love?

He stared through the glass panes separating him from the rest of the staff on the floor. Half his team had taken the day off, or left early—the place was a bit of a ghost town.

He rose, slung the bag over his shoulder, and strode out of his office, shutting the door behind him. He paused at Juliette's desk. "Why don't you go on home too? Nothing further to be done here this afternoon. Monday's another day. Go and enjoy the celebrations. I believe there are several happening around town."

"Thank you, Charles. I appreciate that. Are you planning to go to any of them?"

He nodded. "I'm taking my wife and son to Rolland Moore Park."

An awkward silence hung between them. Charles turned to go. "Well, have a great weekend."

"You too," she called after him.

Faith's car wasn't in the driveway when Charles pulled his Lexus to a stop. Odd. Unless she'd parked it in the garage for some reason or other. He strode in through the front door. "Faith... Michael... I'm home."

Silence echoed a response.

Charles spotted the blanket on the kitchen counter. No basket though. Maybe Faith had run to the store to get something she was missing. Maybe she was planning to put something together during this hour so that it was fresh. He *was* an hour early.

He opened the refrigerator to pour himself a drink and grab a bite to eat in the meantime. Having skipped lunch, he was quite famished. Seeing the picnic basket perched on the middle shelf, Charles cracked a smile. He should have known Faith would be prepared. He took the basket out of the fridge and placed it on the counter beside the blanket. Unable to resist, he peeked inside. Yum!

Well, he had the food and the blanket, but where were his wife and son? Annoyance tapped at the door of his heart but he refused to answer temptation's call to get angry. An idea popped into his mind—forget the stupid picnic and return to the office. He chose to ignore that too. Faith had gone to so much trouble, the least he could do was cut her some slack, extend a little grace. Isn't that what he'd read in the Bible last night? That love is patient and love is kind. That it's not easily angered, and keeps no record of wrongs. He'd made a particular note to remember the verses because that was such a weak area for him lately. He wasn't patient; he wasn't kind; and he got uptight far too easily for way too many small things. He had to work on those areas of his life; he had to change.

Returning to the refrigerator, he grabbed the bottle of milk and the slab of cheese. He poured himself a glass of the white liquid then cut a few slices of yellow goodness. He grabbed a box of crackers from the pantry, then tipped a few out onto a side plate. He covered the crackers with the cheese.

While he waited for Faith, he might as well get out of his suit and into some casual clothes, ones more suitable for a picnic. He quickly finished his snack and headed down the passage.

In the bedroom, Charles took off his suit jacket and hung it on a hanger. As he did, his hand brushed against the pocket. Hello...what was inside there? Charles dug his hand into the pocket and pulled out his cell phone. He'd shoved it in there during that last meeting and forgotten all about it.

As he changed the phone from silent mode, Charles noticed a

missed call from Faith and the subsequent voice message.

"Charles, it's Faith…" Silence, and then a mutter, "Of course you know it's Faith. Anyway, I popped down to Rolland Moore Park to stroll through the various stalls and somehow I've gotten roped in to helping out with a crisis at the church's cupcake stall. Anyway, I wanted you to know in case you're looking for me because I'm turning my phone to silent. Don't worry, I'll be home before you. Michael is already here somewhere with the Hamiltons. We'll meet up with him here. See you soon. And honey, thank you for coming today. It means the world to us. I love you."

If he hurried, he could probably beat her to it—meet her there instead.

Charles quickly exchanged the rest of his business attire for a pair of jeans, a red golf polo shirt, and camel-colored leather boat shoes. He folded the collar of the shirt down then smoothed some gel through his hair to spike it a little. Michael liked it when he wore it that way. "Looks cool, Dad," he'd exclaim.

After slapping fresh cologne around his neck, Charles grabbed the basket and blanket from the kitchen and headed for his car.

There seemed to be no end to the steady stream of customers at the church's stall. On the bright side, at this rate they'd run out of cupcakes soon enough. Faith glanced at her wristwatch. Two thirty. Twenty minutes over the allotted time she'd said she'd help. But every chance she took to get out of there, Cecelia would shush her and plunk another box into her hands. She would give it ten minutes more, then she was ripping off that apron and hightailing it home. So long as she got out of there by quarter to three, she'd be fine.

The last of the cupcakes before her sold, Faith turned to indicate she needed another box. Cecelia's usual post beside their dwindling stack of supplies was empty. She must have gone to the bathroom.

Faith quickly stepped to the back of the stall and wrapped her hands around another two boxes. Only half a dozen still remained. Thankfully she'd thought to keep a few cupcakes for her picnic basket at home. She'd drop a donation into the church's Colorado Day coffers a little later.

She set the boxes down on the serving table, and as she began to open one, a shadow loomed in front of her.

"Those look delicious!"

Her head snapped up at Grayson's voice. What was he doing here? Why wasn't he managing his coffee shop?

His mouth curved in an alluring smile, that gorgeous dimple appearing. "Your handiwork?"

She nodded, trying to restrain her galloping heart. "With Becky's help."

"Well, I'll take two. A pink one and a blue, thank you."

Pink and blue? She raised her gaze to look past his shoulder, her eyes skirting the surrounds. Must have some bimbo here with him. Somewhere.

She fulfilled his request, and pushed the two requested cupcakes toward him. Then she handed him two paper napkins.

"Would you mind turning around?" he asked, his voice low.

"What?"

"I asked if you would mind turning around."

What was he up to?

Faith hesitated a moment before asking why.

"Trust me. You won't be sorry."

She had nothing to lose. Wasn't like he could do anything to her with all these people standing around, not to mention the table separating them.

Faith did a one eighty, then felt a tug on the waist bow of her apron strings. The ties fell loosely at her sides.

"You can turn back now," Grayson instructed.

She complied.

He reached a hand to Faith's neck and slid the apron's loop over her head. The protective garment came away as Grayson pulled his hand back. He dumped the apron on the table. "I'm sorry, but she has to go," he said to the woman helping beside Faith.

Grabbing the two cupcakes, Grayson tipped his head in the direction of the exit. "Meet you outside?"

Too astonished to argue, Faith muttered an apology to her coworker. "I really do have to leave." She grabbed her handbag from under the table and hurried out of the stall.

Grayson waited on the other side of the canvas tent. He handed the pink cupcake to Faith. "I bet you haven't even tried one yet."

Faith shook her head, then ventured a look into his chocolatey gaze, her mind returning not only to the sweet iced coffee they'd all enjoyed together yesterday, but to the times he'd held that same look in his eye and whispered 'I love you.'

"I–I really do have to go. Charles will be home any—"

"One cupcake…with an old friend. Then you're free to leave."

One cupcake. Five minutes. Couldn't hurt. And she sure could do with the sugar rush the frosting promised.

They sat down on a nearby bench, and soon sank their teeth into the sweet topping, following through to the soft, moist cake below.

"Mmm, these are good," Grayson said after he swallowed the first mouthful. "I should get you to bake them on a regular basis for Screamin' Beans."

Faith laughed. "I already have a full-time job. But thanks anyway."

His eyes widened. "You look great by the way." He leaned a little closer. "And if you don't mind me saying so, you smell amazing too."

Mind? When had she last been complimented like that?

Their eyes locked.

"I have missed you so much, Faith. Didn't realize just how much until I saw you again at the movies. I can't stop thinking about you."

"Don't, Grayson. Please. I'm married."

"Happily?"

"I—" Her cheeks warmed. "That isn't any of your business or concern."

She stared at the half-eaten cupcake in her hand, suddenly leaden, its sweet appeal lost. "I should go."

She shoved to her feet.

Grayson remained seated, staring up at her, his last question still burning in his eyes.

"Faith!"

Faith's blood chilled at the sound of her husband calling her name.

CHAPTER SIX

AS FAITH whirled around, Charles's gaze flitted between the cupcake in her hand and the one in the hand of the stranger on the bench. Who was this man his wife was talking to? Was he a stranger, or did they know each other? He'd seen them laughing together as he'd approached.

And what was up with the his and hers cupcakes?

Well, whoever he was, whatever was going on here, he'd show this guy who Faith belonged to.

Charles rushed closer and set the basket and blanket down on the grass. "Hello, my darling." He swept Faith into his arms, and then kissed her like he hadn't done in a very long time.

And strangely, he liked it.

A lot.

His thudding heart bore testament.

"Charles..." Faith said when he finally released her. She sputtered a half laugh. "What are you doing here? I thought you were getting off work at three."

"I wanted to surprise you. When I got home and saw the basket and blanket and got your message, I decided to hurry on over here, hoping to catch you before you left." He splayed his hands and smiled wide. "Surprise!"

Charles turned to Faith's cupcake buddy. "Aren't you going to introduce me, honey?"

"Oh. Yes. Of course. Charles, this is Grayson Fuller, an old friend from high school. Grayson, my husband, Charles."

She seemed nervous. Why?

Grayson slowly rose from the bench, standing taller than Charles as he straightened.

Charles resisted the urge to narrow his eyes and scrutinize the guy. Instead, he stuck out his hand. "Old school friend, huh? So you guys just happened to bump into each other here? At the cupcake stand, I presume?" Out the corner of his eye, Charles noticed Faith encircle her fingers around her cupcake. The pink frosting disappeared in her palm. Seemed as if the thing was scorching a hole in her hand.

She offered a flustered smile. "Yes. Isn't that amazing?"

Charles nodded. "It is. High school...must be what..." He quickly did the math. "Twenty-two years ago? A lifetime." His question hung in the air as his gaze shifted between Faith and her male friend.

"Actually, we lost touch eighteen years ago during Faith's last year at college," Grayson said. "When I left Fort Collins."

Eighteen years. Not long before he had met Faith.

Interesting.

"So what brings you back here?" Charles tried his utmost not to sound jealous. But deep inside, he was burning up. Could this be the guy who'd broken Faith's heart? The one she'd never wanted to talk about when she'd resisted dating Charles after they'd first met. All she had ever said was that she'd had her heart broken badly, and that she never wanted to go through something like that again. It had taken loads of chocolates and flowers and crazy expressions of love to slowly get her to fall for him.

"Business. And family." Grayson's voice pulled Charles from his short trip down memory lane. "I have a son. And Faith is his math teacher."

"Really?" How convenient. "And a wife to go with that son?"

"Charles," Faith whispered and shot him a look.

Charles watched Grayson shake his head. He didn't want to admit it, but this old friend of Faith's was one good-looking fellow.

"Faibian's mother and I never married. It would have been a mistake." Grayson drew Faith into a hug. "Well, it was great seeing you again. You're looking wonderful... Unlike me, married life must suit you."

Charles would love to wipe that smile from Grayson's face. The blood splatters wouldn't be noticeable on his red shirt, would they?

Grayson slowly turned to Charles and shook his hand once again. "It was good to meet you. Enlightening." That said, he strode away, munching on the rest of his cupcake, seemingly pleased with himself.

Enlightening? What had Faith told this friend about him? About their marriage?

He resisted the urge to ask. He had vowed to have a good time today with his wife and son; confound it if he'd let some ex-boyfriend spoil things for them.

Faith's heart pounded, and her temples throbbed. What had Charles seen? Or better put, what had he thought he'd seen?

Charles stared at her and smiled. "Do you want to walk around, or should we find Michael and grab a picnic spot?"

"I walked around earlier. I know how much you dislike strolling from one stall to another. Besides, there's more stuff for me to look at than you. But why don't we first find a spot to sit, preferably close to the stage? There are bands playing from around five. Once we've done that, I'll call Hazel and ask her to let Michael know where we're sitting." The sooner Michael got there, the less chance there'd be of the usual awkward silences that had become their norm.

And less chance of Charles asking about Grayson.

Charles tucked the blanket under his arm then lifted the picnic basket. "Sure, but why don't we have a little time to ourselves first?" He slipped his free hand into hers.

Time to themselves? That was unexpected.

Faith smiled up at him, her gaze searching his bright blue eyes. "I'd like that very much." As long as Grayson did not become the topic of conversation.

Finding an open patch of grass right in front of the stage, Charles spread out the blanket. They sank down on the plaid square.

For the next hour, they chatted about anything and everything. Except Grayson. He'd become the elephant in the park. Grayson aside, they hadn't talked like that in far too long. Somehow, conversation seemed to flow easily. What was happening here? Had God answered her many prayers? Or had a little jealousy gone a long way to make Charles wake up and smell the cupcakes?

Perhaps both things had happened today.

The fact that Charles *hadn't* mentioned Grayson again after he'd left, spoke louder than if her husband had bombarded Faith with questions about her old boyfriend. She knew Charles so well, and the encounter with her ex had definitely affected him. Had Charles realized who Grayson really was? Should she tell him?

Faith twisted her upper body around to watch a band setting up, readying themselves to entertain.

"Penny for your thoughts," Charles said.

"Just thinking about how wonderful this afternoon has been—sitting here with you, talking. It feels good. We haven't done that much lately." Faith lowered her gaze to the blanket and brushed her hand across the soft fibers. "Michael notices what's going on. This morning he asked me if you and I were getting a divorce."

"A divorce? What did you say?"

Faith looked up and held Charles's gaze. "I told him that I believed things were about to change. For the better."

Charles brushed a finger over her cheek before sweeping her hair behind her ear. His Adam's apple bobbed up and down as he swallowed hard. "I'm sorry for the way I've been. I am working on it."

Faith nodded as a guitar chord struck, and the first band began to play.

"I should call Hazel." She grabbed her cell phone from her bag then pushed to her feet. "I won't be long. Why don't you put out some food and drinks for us in the meantime? You know Michael, he's always hungry. He'll be looking for food when he gets here. Honestly, I'm rather famished myself."

Faith hurried away from the loud country music to find a quieter spot to make the call. By the time she got back to Charles, he had dished up three plates of food and poured three glasses of soda. Her heart soared. It felt so good to see glimpses of the man she'd fallen in love with almost eighteen years ago. She had faith that God could warm Charles's heart toward her again.

Sitting down, Faith claimed one of the plates. "Michael's on his way. Thanks for dishing up."

"You're welcome. I left the cupcakes inside the basket. Maybe we can find a stall that sells coffee later? Those little treats of yours will taste even better with a hot drink."

She smiled at Charles. "I couldn't agree more. And I did see a few stalls when I wandered through the park earlier."

"Charlie!" A pretty, petite woman in her late twenties, her long ebony hair tied in a high ponytail, bounced toward them. "I wondered if I'd see you here."

Charlie? Who on earth was this woman?

Charles turned to Faith, and she willed away her frown.

"Faith, you haven't met my secretary yet, have you?" He spoke loud enough to be heard above the music. "This is Juliette. Juliette, my wife, Faith."

Faith rolled onto her knees and stretched out her hand to shake Juliette's. "It's so nice to meet you." Why didn't she know that Charles had such an attractive secretary? She should visit his office more often.

Juliette smiled, perky and wide. "Likewise. So, are you enjoying the celebrations?" She peered into their open picnic basket. "Ooh, cupcakes! I went to the Baptist church stall to get some—a friend had told me how amazing they were—but they were all sold out." Her fuchsia pink lips puffed into a pout.

Faith took two from the basket. "Please, have these. I have more than enough for Charles, Michael, and myself."

Her big blue eyes brightened. "Really? Thank you. My friends will have to fight over the spare one. I'm having this yellow one all to myself."

She turned to go then paused. "It was nice to finally meet you, Mrs. Young. Charlie, see you in the office on Monday." With a giggle she hurried off into the gathering crowd.

"Charlie?" Faith raised a questioning brow.

Charles lifted his shoulders. "No idea where that comes from. If I didn't know better, I'd say she's lingered too long at the craft beer stalls with her friends."

From the raised platform, the lead singer held the final note while the banjo player finished the song with a few last plucks of the strings.

The crowd that had gathered on the grass clapped and cheered.

"Thank you, everybody!" The microphone gave a screech, and the lead singer took a step away from the mic stand.

Another man, dressed in cowboy boots, blue jeans, and a white cotton shirt, the sleeves rolled up, rushed to the center of the platform. "Let's hear it for the Anderson Brothers."

The band took one last bow then left the stage.

"Good afternoon, fellow Coloradans. I'm Austin Landon, and I'll be introducing the various acts today," Cowboy Boots said. "Next up we have another local act, born and bred right here in Fort Collins. Since he's been away from our beautiful college town for so long, I'm not sure how many of you will still remember him. That said, he recently returned and opened the popular Screamin' Beans Coffee Shop where I believe you won't get a better cup of hot, fresh brew. Let's give a hearty FoCo welcome to…" Austin dragged out the word. "Grayson… Fuller."

"Seriously?" Charles muttered, his expression darkening. "Is he going to be everywhere we go today?"

"I—"

Spotting Faith, Grayson smiled. Then again, how could he miss her?—she was sitting almost right under his nose. He pulled a high bar stool closer then sat, one leg extended, foot firmly planted on the wooden platform while he perched his other foot on the metal support. Grayson rested his guitar on his thigh and began to strum.

"Mom! Dad!" Michael skidded to his knees on the blanket, a welcome interruption. He stretched out his hand to grab the ham and cheese roll from the untouched plate. He bit into the soft bread like a Neanderthal. "Yum, this looks good. I'm so hungry."

"Michael, how many times have I told you not to speak with a mouth full of food?" Faith admonished.

"Sorry, Mom." Bread, ham, and cheese swirled around Michael's words.

Boys!

Michael plunked onto his backside, crossed his legs, and focused on the stage. "Wow, this dude is good. Just listen to his voice."

Grayson was. How had she not known he could play the guitar and had a voice like that? Or was that something he'd picked up post-Faith Peterson days?

Michael sighed. "Wish I could sing like that."

Faith smiled at her son. He probably would, once he got through puberty.

> *...and I messed up, baby, with you.*
> *Why, oh why couldn't I be true?*
> *If I got a chance again,*
> *to make things right again,*
> *I'd pack my bags again*
> *and run away*
> *Only this time I'd run*
> *right back to you...*
>
> *My papa always said,*
> *"Boy, you gotta have a little faith.*
> *You gotta believe in something,*
> *you gotta have faith, my son,*
> *can't believe in nothing.*
> *Gotta have faith*
> *to get you through..."*
> *So I'll choose to have a little faith,*
> *darlin' in me and you...*

CHAPTER SEVEN

PARKED OUTSIDE Screamin' Beans for more than ten minutes already, Faith sat glued behind the steering wheel. She turned her phone around in her hands—over and over. Her better judgment told her she should cancel the lunch date, but she just couldn't bring herself to do it. She really wanted to help Faibian—poor boy had endured enough of a raw deal growing up with an almost nonexistent father. To still go through life struggling with mathematics…? Besides, she did want to question Grayson in person about the song he'd sung at the Colorado Day celebrations. It had replayed in her mind for almost six days now. Had he written it for her? About her? Or were the similarities to their story purely coincidental?

Did it even matter?

It shouldn't, but…

The idea that Charles was having an affair with his secretary had also churned in her mind. Surely he wouldn't? And yet, she couldn't ignore the timing. Charles had started to become distant from Faith probably around the time his new secretary, Juliette, had started working for him.

She shoved the notion aside and opened the driver's door. She couldn't think about that now. First she had to get this lunch with Grayson and the discussion about his son's tutoring over with. As quickly as was possible.

As Faith entered the coffee shop, Grayson looked up from behind the serving counter. Drat, she'd kept him waiting by wasting time sitting there in her car, undecided.

An awful thought hit her. Did he see her car parked outside?

She turned to look through the large windows. Of course he could see her car. Then he had to know how long ago she'd arrived.

Jaw set, she lifted her chin, firming her resolve. She didn't owe him any explanation. She wasn't *that* late. Dash it, let him think what he wanted. She could have been on a phone call for all he knew.

Grayson strolled toward her, as if he hadn't noticed she was late. "I'm glad you made it. I've reserved a booth for us. Shall we?" He held out his arm for Faith.

She declined to take him up on his offer, walking half a step ahead of him toward the empty booth, instead. She slid onto the curved bench.

Grayson took his place on the other side of the table, his gaze not leaving her. "You look stunning."

Really? She'd deliberately avoided any hip-hugging jeans or dresses that showed too much skin. Instead, she'd chosen pale-blue cotton slacks and matching jacket with a white button-up blouse beneath. One of the outfits she wore in the classroom.

"You hungry?" he asked.

She had been. But somewhere between parking her car and walking inside, she'd lost her appetite.

"Not extremely. I'll maybe just have a salad, if you have those on the menu." Something light would do the trick.

He grinned, and she wished he wouldn't. That dimple had to go.

"We have a smoked chicken salad with mango and avocado," he said. "It's really delicious. I think you'll like it."

"Great. I'll have one of those, with a sparkling water. Please."

Grayson ordered two of the same then relaxed into his seat, spreading one arm out across the backrest.

Faith averted her gaze from the muscular arm on display. She should skip any small talk and get right down to business.

"So, I've given tutoring Faibian a lot of thought, and I'd really like to help him further."

"Can you start tomorrow?"

Faith gulped. "To–morrow? It's summer vacation—what would Faibian think about having to take more math classes during the break?"

"He's reluctantly on board with the idea, but nevertheless grateful that you are prepared to consider helping him more."

"Oh. I'd envisaged the extra tutoring would only happen during the school term. This does raise some concerns for me, but I'm sure we'll find a way to address them."

Grayson leaned forward and clasped his hands together on the table. His brow furrowed. "Concerns? What concerns?"

"Where would I teach him during the holidays? I don't have access to the school, and it wouldn't be wise to tutor him at my house, or yours for that matter." She shook her head. "A young man and me alone... Even though I know nothing would happen except algebra and trigonometry, it's best to keep away from any appearance of evil, don't you think?"

"Oh, yes." Grayson's serious look quickly gave way to a chuckle, laughter lines appearing around his eyes.

"I'm serious, Grayson."

"I know you are! That's what's so funny."

Just then their waiter arrived with their salads and waters. He set the two plates, glasses, and bottled waters down in front of them then left.

Grayson cracked the bottles and poured them each a glass. He eased farther forward. "Why don't you bring him here? Would that work?"

She shook her head. "Too noisy. Too many distractions."

"You could use my office in the back. I can even have a chalkboard installed for you."

That would mean seeing Grayson every time she tutored Faibian. But it would likely not be more than twice a week. And it was only for the summer vacation, which was almost over, anyway.

"All right. How about every Tuesday and Thursday here in your office? We can start next week. That gives you four days to get that board up. Once school resumes, we'll continue the extra lessons in my classroom immediately after the school day ends."

"Deal. Do you want me to pay you per lesson, or monthly?"

Faith shrugged. "It really doesn't matter. Whatever works best for you."

"And your rates?"

Faith smiled and giggled. "Oh, a million bucks per lesson. Hope you can afford that."

His eyes widened. "I knew you were good, but can anyone be *that* good?"

"Guess you're about to find out." She reached out to reassure him, then paused, quickly diverting her hand toward the glass of water. She took a long drink.

"Don't worry," Faith said as she set her glass down. "I'll be gentle on the billing."

Conversation decreased as they plowed through their salad. Again, Grayson wasn't kidding—this salad was delicious.

When they'd finished their meal, Grayson offered Faith a

coffee. She gladly accepted, on the proviso it was a hot cappuccino.

The coffees were soon delivered, complete with a heart pattern sprinkled into the foam on each cup. They both noticed, and they both began to laugh.

"Are you responsible for that?" Faith asked as her chuckles ceased. She lifted the cup and took a sip. Amazing coffee. She should ask Grayson what brand they used, get some for home.

"Not guilty, although I do wish I'd been the one to think of that." Grayson's gaze grew serious. "Are you happily married, Faith?"

Here he was, a week later, asking that same question. Were her and Charles's problems that obvious? If only she was able to lie to him. But she couldn't. Besides, Grayson had always been good at reading her; he'd probably still be able to tell if she wasn't truthful.

"We're...going through something at the moment."

"Charles must be in his forties, probably? Midlife crisis, perhaps?"

"Maybe, I don't know."

"Has he bought any sports cars? Motorbikes? Had an affair?"

She shook her head. "No! Nothing like that." *Please, don't press me any further.*

Grayson reached across the table, his hand on Faith's reassuring her. "If you ever need anything, I'm here for you. I was such a fool to have ever let you go. I've never stopped loving you, Faith."

Faith yanked her hand out from under his. "I–I need to go."

His hand shot out to stop her. "Do you know why I named my son Faibian?"

She frowned. How would she know why?

"The first three letters of his name are the same as yours," Grayson continued, determined to be heard despite the fact that Faith had once again escaped his grasp and had already retrieved her handbag from the seat beside her. "I never wanted to forget you—always wanted to have something to remind me of you."

"Grayson...don't." She shot to her feet. "Thank you for lunch."

As Faith headed for the door, Grayson followed right behind, shadowing her.

At the car, she fumbled inside her bag for her keys. Where were they when she needed them in a hurry?

Grayson positioned himself in front of her. "Faith, I'm sorry. I shouldn't have."

She glanced up at him. "No, you shouldn't have. You were out of line." She lowered her gaze back to the open bag.

"I know. And I *am* sorry. Forgive me?"

Fingers beneath her chin, he tipped her head up. He did look contrite, but was he merely worried she'd refuse to tutor Faibian now?

She drew in a deep breath to compose herself. "It's all right. No harm done."

"Thank you."

Faith returned to rummaging in her bag. Her keys seemed to have vanished.

"Looking for these." Grayson dangled a familiar set of keys in front of her nose.

"Wh— Where did you get those?"

"You left them on the table. Along with your cell phone." He dug in his pocket and pulled out her phone. He placed the keys and phone in her hands, and their skin touched once more as he did. Faith could no longer deny the attraction, the sparks that still existed between them after all these years.

She unlocked the car. "I have to go."

"Wait." Grayson's gaze held hers. He shook his head from side to side and snorted. "You know what. I'm not sorry. You're not happy, and I should have done this a week ago." He pulled her into his arms and into his kiss, and for one momentary lapse, Faith forgot she was no longer twenty-two, forgot she was no longer single.

The meeting at Beaumont, Hadley & Co. had gone on far longer than Charles had anticipated. Still, he had an hour to spare, and he was starving. He'd look for a place to have lunch before heading back to the office. He rounded the corner and began searching for a restaurant or takeout the moment he stepped onto the main street.

Across the road from where he walked sat Colorado State University, quiet, void of the thousands of students that usually milled around the grounds each day. Wouldn't be like that for much longer. In a few weeks, the education system would resurrect, the core of their community jump-started by the commencement of the new school year. Just like a heart receiving life-giving doses of electrical currents through the paddles of a defibrillator, Fort Collins would throb, bustle, and come alive once again.

He, for one, couldn't wait. Every night when he got home, he heard from Michael about how bored he'd been that day. Faith, too, seemed eager to get back to her students.

Speaking of, was that her car up ahead? Maybe he should call her, take her out for lunch.

As Charles neared, he saw Faith exit a building. He glanced at the overhead signage. Screamin' Beans. Wasn't that the place belonging to that singer school friend of hers?

He was about to call Faith's name when Grayson Fuller trotted into view, hot on Faith's heels. Grayson followed Faith to her car.

Charles ducked behind a large tree. Leaning against the thick trunk, he carefully peered around the side, keeping Faith and Grayson just in sight. They were talking, and he watched them keenly for a minute before Grayson took Faith in his arms and kissed her.

Nausea rushed up Charles's throat. He looked away, his eyes darting in search of a trash can. Any minute now he was going to throw up all over the pavement. He breathed in and out, slow and deep. So this was why his marriage wasn't working. Faith was having an affair. He'd been a fool. He should've seen the writing on the wall last Friday. When he'd stumbled upon Faith and Grayson enjoying their little cupcake date in the park, they had both looked guilty. Especially Faith.

Yanking on his tie, Charles loosened it. By the time he glanced back, Faith's car had pulled out of the parking space. It grew smaller as she drove away. Grayson remained rooted, his back toward Charles, watching her depart. Then he strode back inside his coffee shop.

Charles balled his hands into fists. He should march down there right now and punch Grayson Fuller's head right off his shoulders. Instead, Charles slumped against the tree. What would a fist-fight help? It would only serve to further alienate Faith, although at this point, he wasn't certain he wanted to save his marriage. But he didn't want Grayson to have her either. However, did he stand a fighting chance against the guy? Grayson Fuller was way bigger than him, and far more good-looking.

He needed a drink. Not that he really drank—the occasional glass of wine or a beer. Right now though, he needed something to calm his nerves.

Charles stumbled back to his car, thoughts of food long forgotten. He drove aimlessly through town, finally stopping at a hotel on the outskirts of town. He entered and headed straight to the bar.

By the time Charles was sipping his fourth drink, his head beginning to swirl, he'd formulated a plan. Sort of. Hadn't his father always taught him not to get mad but to get even? Despite Charles's vow never to pass the teaching on to Michael, maybe his father had been right. And he could certainly play the same dirty game as Faith.

He pulled his cell phone from his jacket pocket and dialed.

A sweet, familiar voice answered.

"Mr. Young's office, good afternoon. Juliette speaking, how can I assist you?"

Charles sucked in a breath. Here went nothing. And everything. Here went sweet revenge. "Juliette, Charles here."

"Charles, where are you? I've been trying to contact you for the past hour." Juliette sounded perplexed.

Should he confess that he'd ignored her calls?

He chose to remain silent.

"You missed your three thirty meeting with the finance director," Juliette continued.

Charles swore under his breath. That meeting was important—problems he was having on one client's account—and he'd forgotten all about it.

"Please give his secretary my apologies. Something urgent…a family crisis…came up."

Juliette's gasp sounded through the phone. "Is everything all right?"

No, everything was not all right. Things may never be right again. He downed the remaining amber liquid. It warmed his insides, dulling his senses a little more. He just wanted to forget what he'd witnessed earlier.

And he desperately wanted to get even.

"It will be. Please try to reschedule with Mr. Martins for Monday morning."

"I'll do so right away, boss. Anything else you need done?"

"Yes. I need you to contact my wife. Tell her I had to leave at one for a conference in Denver and that I'll be back tomorrow evening."

"Conference? What conference?"

Charles indicated to the barman to fill his glass again—a double shot this time.

"Just tell her, Juliette! No questions asked!"

That was harsh. There was no need to take this out on her.

"I–I'm sorry, Juliette. That was uncalled for. It's just... I'm going through something right now. Something bad."

"Where are you? Sounds like you could do with that listening ear I offered you recently."

It would be nice to talk to someone. And he couldn't talk to Jackson like this—half intoxicated. Juliette wouldn't judge either.

Charles shifted his glass over and picked up the branded coaster it had rested on. He read out the name of the hotel printed on the thin, four-inch-square cork then said goodbye. He muted his phone and shoved it into his jacket pocket, along with the coaster, before taking another swig of Scotch.

CHAPTER EIGHT

FAITH RELEASED a heavy sigh as she shut the front door of her home behind her. Tears stinging, she fell with her back against the door and closed her eyes. She should tell Charles what had happened with Grayson, but just the thought made her nauseous. Besides, what purpose would that serve? Their marriage was already on shaky ground—telling Charles would only make things a million times worse. Her husband simply wouldn't understand.

What if he thought she was the one responsible, that she'd initiated the kiss or asked for it? Worse, if she told him about the kiss, he could be swayed to thinking that she and Grayson were having an affair. And heaven forbid *that* thought ever wormed its way into his mind. Their marriage would have zero chance of survival if it did.

She glanced at her wristwatch then pushed away from the door and headed into the kitchen, the house deathly quiet. As usual. Michael had gone to Jeremy's house, and Charles was still at work. He'd return soon though, so she should start with dinner preparations.

Goodness, where had the afternoon gone?

She knew exactly where. It had whiled away as she'd driven aimlessly through the streets of Fort Collins, finally pulling her station wagon to a stop under the trees beside Horsetooth Reservoir. She'd taken a walk out on the jetty and poured her heart out to her Heavenly Father as she'd stared across the dark blue waters. She'd begged for forgiveness over what had transpired that afternoon, and she'd pleaded with God to save her marriage. But the peace that had descended in those moments of prayer, had quickly dissipated the moment she'd arrived back home.

Faith reached for her cookbook standing on a metal book stand on her kitchen counter. She flipped through the section filled with chicken recipes, trying to decide what she'd do with those thighs she'd taken out of the freezer early that morning. Michael was sleeping over at Jeremy's tonight. She would make Charles a delicious dinner—food was the way to a man's heart, or so the saying went—and after dinner she'd tell him about Grayson. She couldn't keep secrets from her husband; they would only come back to bite her later.

A ringing from her handbag gave her pause. Leaving the cookbook open, she grasped her bag from where she'd dumped it at one end of the kitchen counter. She unzipped the bag and searched for her phone, earlier memories of Grayson's kiss that had followed a similar bag rummaging flooding her mind. She touched her lips as she answered the call.

"Faith Young."

The fragrance of a familiar perfume drifted toward Charles. He gave a sideways glance as Juliette slid onto the bar stool beside him. Was she really here to offer her ear alone? Only problem was, over the course of the last two Scotches, he'd progressed from desiring a listening ear to desperately needing a shoulder to cry on.

"You look rough." She offered a sympathetic smile.

"And you look fantasssshtic." Maybe he should forget the shoulder to cry on. Juliette had a whole lot more to offer.

"Thanks… I think." She tipped her head to one side. "You want to talk, Charles?"

He tried to focus his gaze on her. Didn't help much; her image remained a blur. "Charlesssh? What happened to Charlie?"

Had he just slurred his words?

Juliette narrowed her brows, and tiny lines formed on her forehead. "Charlie? I–I don't understand."

"Lassst Friday, at the park…you called me Charlie. Been meaning to assshk you about that, young lady." One too many drinks tonight had definitely given him the courage to do so now.

Juliette laughed. "I'm sorry. I don't remember. Can we just put that down to the fact I'd probably tested one too many craft beers that afternoon and leave it at that?"

"Sshure." Charles smiled at her, probably a silly grin, and returned to his drink. He swigged back the rest of the glass's contents then called the bartender over. "Hit me with another."

"I–I think you've had enough for one night," Juliette intervened. "Can you bring me two coffees instead?"

She turned to Charles. "That is, if you don't mind? I'm afraid I won't be able to get you home if you have any more to drink."

The barman's attention shifted from Juliette to Charles. "So, coffee or Scotch?"

Charles chuckled. The solution was easy. "Can I have an Irisssh coffee?"

"No, you may not." A smile tugged at Juliette's lips. "I think you've had more than enough whiskey for one night. If you're not careful, I'll change the order to a black coffee instead."

Ugh. He hated black coffee, and Juliette knew that. She must mean business. Best he toe the line with her.

"Coffee issh good." And she was right on one thing. He *had* consumed enough for the night. Already, the promise of a headache tomorrow morning loomed. He didn't need to make things worse.

Juliette took his hand in hers. "Why don't you tell me what's going on over that cup of coffee?"

Why wait for coffee?

"I've blown thingsss with my wife. Forced her into another man's armsss through my actionsss." Charles fell against her shoulder and sobbed. "I ssshould have treated her better."

"Are you sure you've messed up?"

His head moved up and down against the soft fabric of her blouse.

"There must be a logical explanation. And you... I couldn't imagine you treating anyone badly."

"Oh, I did. For far too long." He'd been such a jerk. So stupid. For what? Some other guy to swoop in and meet Faith's needs, desires, and wants as a woman?

For a few minutes, Juliette wrapped Charles in a consoling hug. "I should get you home. How about I drive you, and tomorrow when you're sober, we can return to collect your car. I'd be happy to help."

Charles sat upright. "Home? No! I can't go home like this. Besssidesss, Faith thinks I'm down in Denver at a conference, remember? You did call her and tell her that, didn't you?"

Juliette nodded. She pushed to her feet with a sigh. "All right. You win. Wait here and I'll check you into the hotel for the night. Just don't drink anything while I'm gone. Only coffee."

Charles sat nursing his cup when Juliette returned. She slid a key card over to him then took a sip of her coffee. She exhaled. "Thankfully, it's still warm. Nothing worse than cold coffee."

He glanced at the number. Three ten. Third floor? Would he

make it?

He cleared his throat. "Um, would you mind helping me to my room?" Without aid, he feared his unsteady legs might not get him all the way there.

Juliette held his gaze. "Of course. I did tell you before that I'd do anything for you."

There was that word again. What exactly did she mean by anything?

Did he even want to find out?

Long, manicured fingers reached for the key card to retrieve it, and Juliette helped Charles to his feet. As they navigated the route to the elevators, she allowed him to lean against her. Juliette slid the key card into the lock of room three ten, and the door clicked open.

A conference? In Denver? Faith still couldn't get her head around the notion, despite the fact that hours had passed since Charles's secretary had called to inform her of this sudden business commitment.

She packed the freshly washed and folded clothes away in her and Charles's closets then returned to the kitchen. She stared out of the window to the back garden. Something didn't make sense. Why hadn't Charles been told about this long ago? She should've asked Juliette, but Faith had been so taken aback with the news, she hadn't had time to process the information.

She'd tried to phone Charles. The call had gone straight to voicemail, but she figured he would've turned off his phone if he was attending a conference.

After leaving a message, Faith had tried his office to find out more from Juliette. That call went to voicemail too. She didn't bother leaving a message that time. Maybe Juliette had taken advantage of the fact that her boss wasn't there and sneaked away early.

Charles must have rushed home to pack an overnight bag while she was out. Her already failing spirits sank even lower. He probably wasn't happy that she hadn't been there to help him pack. If he'd just called to tell her he had to go out of town, she would've gone home immediately. And she would've avoided Grayson's kiss. If only she'd followed her gut not to go to lunch with Grayson today. It had all gone wrong in so many ways.

Faith turned away from the kitchen window. Tempted as she was to invite Becky around to share her lovely but lonely home for a few hours, she chose to return the untouched chicken to the fridge and headed to the bathroom. After a lengthy soak in a bubble bath, she would crawl into bed with her Bible and seek comfort from the Scriptures.

The bath was anything but relaxing. It only served to feed unwanted thoughts—thoughts of how much she'd enjoyed Grayson's attention earlier, not to mention his fleeting kiss. Had she been at all to blame for his action? Had she sent Grayson any signals that she was interested in him beyond the scope of helping his son with his math?

She'd resisted the urge to slap him when he'd kissed her. Instead, she'd pulled herself from his embrace and fell into her car, driving away from him as fast as she could.

But thoughts of Grayson weren't Faith's only unwanted reverie. Her mind swam with confusion about Charles and this conference, about why his secretary was also unavailable, about the pretty young woman affectionately calling her husband Charlie recently. Was there something going on between them that she was oblivious to?

She exhaled a heavy sigh. Wasn't the wife always the last to know if her husband was unfaithful?

Tears tumbled down Faith's cheeks, mixing with the bathwater, as she faced the harsh reality that perhaps Charles was having an affair.

Dried and dressed in her pajamas, Faith knelt beside her bed. Clasping her hands in prayer, she poured out her heart. *Father God, protect Charles...wherever he might be tonight, wherever he might go. Please, save our marriage...do whatever it takes.*

CHAPTER NINE

CHARLES WOKE the following morning to a headache the size of the state of Texas. He lifted his head from the pillow, scrunching his eyes at the bright beam of light shining on his face through a crack in the curtains. The room was warm and muggy.

Ugh, where was he?

He glanced at the unfamiliar bedsheets, before allowing his gaze to take in the equally unaccustomed surroundings. His eyes froze on his clothes hanging over a chair beside a desk in the corner of the room. Had he undressed himself? Or had someone helped him?

Charles pushed himself upright in the king-size bed. From the vantage point, he spotted a note lying on the bedside table. He reached for the piece of paper.

Charles, thank you for trusting me last night. I will not break your confidence. Hope you don't feel too worse for wear this morning. Be assured I will cover for you at work. And at home. See you on Thursday.

Thursday?

Of course... Juliette. She'd taken three days off next week—going away with friends, she'd said.

He groaned. What had he gotten himself into last night?

An image of him and Juliette filling that bed—whether true or false was anyone's guess—flashed through his mind, and nausea rose. Charles scrambled for the waste basket beside the desk and dumped the contents of his stomach into the metal container. The effects of too much alcohol? Or a guilty conscience?

If only he could remember.

He stumbled to the bathroom. Perhaps his brain would function better after a shower. He could only hope his hangover would ease somewhat with plenty of steam and hot water.

Snippets of the previous day flashed through Charles's mind as he stood rooted under the warm spray. Faith and Grayson, kissing. Glass upon glass of amber liquid. His secretary's comfort through a fuzzy haze. His hotel room. Juliette...

The last thing he remembered—falling onto the bed, dragging Juliette with him. After that, everything was blank.

Charles turned off the taps and stepped out of the glass cubicle. He grabbed one of the soft, white towels and dried himself. Then he dressed in his wrinkled clothes from the previous day, sans jacket and tie.

Looking for a hair dryer, he found a Gideon Bible in the desk drawer. Hands shaking, Charles reached for the Scriptures then sank into the chair that earlier had been a hanger for his clothing. He placed the Bible on the desk and opened it. He began to read Psalm 51.

Have mercy on me, O God, according to Your unfailing love; according to Your great compassion, blot out my transgressions. Wash away all my iniquity and cleanse me from my sin. For I know my transgressions, and my sin is always before me. Against You, You only, have I sinned and done what is evil in Your sight...

Hide Your face from my sins and blot out all my iniquity. Create in me a pure heart, O God, and renew a steadfast spirit within me. Do not cast me from Your presence or take Your Holy Spirit from me. Restore to me the joy of Your salvation and grant me a willing spirit, to sustain me...

My sacrifice, O God, is a broken spirit; a broken and contrite heart You, God, will not despise.

The overwhelming desire to not only read that Psalm, but to pray it, engulfed Charles. Staring at the black words on the thin, white page, he read the verses again, this time out loud as an earnest prayer to God. If David, the adulterer, was a man after God's own heart, surely there was a chance that Charles could enjoy intimate fellowship once again with his Creator? And with his wife. God alone could restore their marriage, but it had to start with him. He had to make right with his Lord first, and then with his wife. Restoration would begin by him seeking God's forgiveness. Then Faith's.

Charles shrugged into his jacket. As he scanned the room for any of his belongings, Juliette's note caught his attention. He folded it twice, then dropped it into his jacket pocket. He'd get rid of that somewhere else.

He gazed at the open Bible. He would need that with him today. Remembering a recent talk in church by the Gideons, Charles shut the Bible with a snap and tucked it beneath his arm before exiting his hotel room, his conscience clear he wasn't stealing. How many people actually knew the Gideons were thrilled when someone kept a Bible?

But, he planned to bring it back—someone else might need it one day. He just wanted to borrow it for a few hours.

After settling his bill, Charles climbed into his car and drove away, putting whatever had happened there behind him. For now. He'd have to deal with those events later.

He veered the Lexus south toward Loveland, the town where he had first fallen in love with Faith. He wanted to remember the good times they'd shared there. Wanted to be drawn back to that first love he'd had for her. Once he'd accomplished that, he'd head into the mountains at Estes Park, and find the first love he'd once had for God too. There was something about the majesty of mountain peaks that seemed to draw a person closer to the Maker of the universe.

Faith rested her palms on the edge of the kitchen sink and stared out the window. She loved this time of the year. The garden looked great, but she should ask Charles to shear the Snowmound spirea at the back of their yard. It hadn't had a heavy pruning in several years and was getting out of hand.

Charles... She'd still not managed to contact him. And he hadn't returned any of her calls. What was going on? Everything about the last two days caused an uneasiness to settle into her bones. Perhaps a cup of hot tea would settle her disquiet.

She pivoted and switched on the kettle before returning to her thoughts. Assuming the conference ended around five, Charles should be home by six thirty at the latest. She glanced at the kitchen clock—two hours more. She'd have faith that he'd be home—just as his secretary had told her—and start with dinner. Michael would be home soon too. She'd given him a five o'clock curfew.

The cookbook still lay open on the counter where she'd left it the previous evening. She continued flipping through the recipes until she found one she was certain would warm her husband's heart.

What had happened this past week? Charles had seemed so loving and attentive at the Colorado Day picnic, but he'd withdrawn to his usual aloof self after Grayson's song. Had he figured out who Grayson was? And did he also think that song had been meant for her? If it had been meant for her, she'd have to knock that notion flat.

She would have to put any suspicions to rest tonight. Once Michael was in bed and they could talk freely.

What an incredible and life-changing day Charles had experienced—retracing his first love for Faith, rekindling his first love for God.

But now he had to face the music back home. Everything. Even the stuff he didn't want to face, himself. He'd made right with God; it was time to make right with his wife.

He turned his SUV left onto Route 34, leaving the majestic Rocky Mountains behind him.

Before he spilled his guts to Faith, though, he should check the facts with Juliette. No use in confessing something to his wife that didn't happen, right? Although Juliette *had* said on more than one occasion that she'd do *anything* for him. Did that include sleeping with him? Had he expected that last night? And had she made good on her offer? Or had she just been what he could remember?—a listening ear and a shoulder to cry on.

Anyone who looks at a woman lustfully has already committed adultery with her in his heart.

Could he argue with that? Even if it turned out that he was innocent of cheating on Faith, could he say with absolute certainty he hadn't thought of his secretary in that way last night? He'd wanted to get even. He'd wanted revenge. So he probably had entertained impure thoughts of Juliette.

He needed to know the truth.

With Juliette out of the office for three days, he tried her cell phone. The call went straight to voicemail. If he didn't manage to contact her, he'd have to delay telling Faith until Thursday when he could sit Juliette down in his office and find out exactly what had transpired last night. On the other hand, it *would* give him five or six days to endear himself to Faith. Perhaps God wanted that to happen first. He'd treated her abysmally the past few years, so telling her he *might* have been unfaithful to her last night may not be quite the right thing to do. Yet.

But what of her unfaithfulness? Had he truly meant it when he'd told God in the mountains that he would forgive her unconditionally, that he wouldn't even mention her indiscretion unless she did?

When the Lexus pulled into their driveway around seven, Michael bolted for the door.

"Dad's home!"

Faith managed a smile for her son as she wiped her hands on her apron. She removed the smock, then smoothed her hands down her blouse, tugging the fabric over her jeans. Did she look good enough for Charles? She hoped so. She'd missed him last night. Hopefully, he'd missed her too. Maybe they'd be able to show each other how much later, once Michael was asleep.

Please, let him welcome my touch, Lord. Let him reciprocate with mind, body, and soul. Not just his body as had become the norm.

She strode to the front door to greet her husband. "You're home." She leaned in to kiss him on the cheek.

"Yeah, I'm home."

As Charles set his laptop bag down on the carpet against the wall, Faith helped him out of his jacket. "Let me take that for you. Are you hungry?"

He grinned, and her heart skipped a beat. There was something different about him. A warmth radiating from his smile.

"I'm beyond hungry. I'm famished."

Michael rubbed his palms together and bounced on his heels. "Me too. Mom's made these amazing chicken thighs, glazed with some kind of Asian sauce. Dad, it smells sooo good, I can't wait to eat."

Faith turned to Michael. "Well, you'll have to wait a little longer, son. I'm sure your dad is tired from the conference and the trip. Let's give him a few minutes to shower and get out of that suit, huh? Looks like the same one he left in yesterday, so I'm sure he'd like to freshen up and change into something more comfortable."

Charles nodded. "I would. Thanks. I won't take long."

Faith gave him a few minutes of privacy before following him to the room to hang up his jacket. His suit pants and shirt lay on the bed. From inside the bathroom, the sound of running water could be heard. She grabbed a wooden hanger from inside Charles's closet then hung his jacket over it. She lifted the pants from the bed and slid them over the rounded bar that formed the bottom part of the hanger's triangle. She buttoned the jacket and smoothed her hands down the fabric, straightening it. Her palm brushed against a bulge in the right pocket.

Charles's phone. He was always shoving it somewhere inside his jacket.

Dipping her hand inside the pocket, Faith's fingers wrapped around the phone. Wait. There was something else in the pocket. She retrieved the phone then went back for the items she'd felt beside it—a coaster and a note. She stared at the coaster from a local hotel. Why would Charles have that in his pocket? And what was the note all about?

She unfolded the piece of paper and read...

Charles, thank you for trusting me last night. I will not break your confidence. Hope you don't feel too worse for wear this morning. Be assured I will cover for you at work. And at home. See you on Thursday.

Her veins chilled. Thursday? Did Charles and the writer of this note hold clandestine tête-à-têtes on Thursdays?

Heart racing, Faith left the suit hanging on the closet doorknob. She dove for the bed and Charles's white button-up shirt. She fumbled it between her fingers, almost instantly finding the pink smudge across the collar.

Didn't matter now that the note was unsigned. She recognized the shade.

Fuchsia pink.

Faith raised her hand to her mouth and gasped. "Dear God, no!" She dug her fingers into her hair then pressed her palms against her skull, willing away the sordid, painful truth. Charles was having an affair with his secretary. He hadn't been in Denver at a conference. He'd been right here in Fort Collins, with that woman.

She grabbed his wallet from where he'd discarded it on his bedside table. With trembling fingers, she rifled through the contents before spilling them onto the bed. Faith examined each credit card slip. When she held the one dated that morning for the same hotel as was printed on the coaster, for an amount equivalent to a night's accommodation, she slid to the floor and buried her head in her knees, and wept.

"Faith...honey... What's wrong?" Charles rushed to her side, sliding a hand across her shoulder. Silence descended for a moment before he spoke again. "I–I can explain. It's not what you think."

Faith raised her head. "Really? So this isn't what I think it is?" She flung the slip in Charles's face then shoved to her feet. She grabbed the white shirt and threw it at him. "And that pink smudge isn't what I think it is?"

"I—" Charles stood and reached for her. "Faith, listen to me. Please."

She recoiled at his touch. "No! I'm not listening to any more of your lies. Y–you slept with your secretary." She held up her hands in surrender. Lowering her gaze, she slowly shook her head. "I'm done. I'm out of this loveless marriage."

If only he hadn't promised God that he wouldn't raise the Grayson issue unless Faith wanted to talk about it. Hard as it was not to, Charles knew if he did, he couldn't say he'd forgiven her. And everything that had happened that afternoon in the mountains between him and God would be questionable. What would that say about his repentance?

All he could do for now was to watch her pack a bag for her and Michael and let her go. He couldn't defend himself against the evidence stacked against him. He had to speak to Juliette urgently, find out what really happened last night. She was the only one who could set the record straight.

Charles prayed those records would prove him innocent, not guilty.

Refusing his help, Faith dragged her suitcase to her car and dumped it in the back. Charles stayed out of her way, looking on through the living room windows—helpless—as his family disintegrated before his eyes. The hard lump that had formed in the back of his throat the moment Faith had accused him almost kept him from breathing.

Michael stared at Charles from the doorway. He swiped at his cheeks then dropped his bag and rushed toward his father. He flung his arms around Charles's neck with a loud sob. "Dad... Please...don't let Mom take us away. Do something."

Charles tightened his grip around his son, his own tears wetting Michael's hair. "I'm so sorry. I never meant to hurt anyone, least of all you. Just give your mom some time; she'll come around, and this whole misunderstanding will be resolved." He offered Michael a weak smile. "You'll see."

"Misunderstanding? What misunderstanding? What happened between you two, Dad?"

Charles ruffled Michael's blond hair. "Don't worry about it, son. Just look after your mom in the meantime. Will you promise me that?"

"I promise, Dad." Michael wrapped his arms around his father again and hugged him hard.

A horn blew twice outside before Faith shouted, "Michael, we have to go."

Charles gave his son a final hug before releasing him.

Michael hurried to the door and picked up his bag. He disappeared through the opening.

Charles rushed to follow him, pausing when he spotted the transparent, plastic tub filled with chicken that Faith had packed for Michael still sitting on the edge of the kitchen counter. He grabbed the tub and ran outside.

Michael had just put his bag in the back of the station wagon and shut the liftgate. His shoulders shook with sobs as he dragged his feet to the passenger door.

"Michael," Charles called, holding up the container. He trotted to the car and handed the food to Michael. "Don't forget this."

Michael latched on to Charles once again. "D–dad... I'm going to miss you."

"Me too, son. Me too." He helped Michael into the car then shut the door. He stuck his head through the open window. "Where will you go?" he asked Faith.

Without looking at him, she shook her head. "I–I don't know. Anywhere but here."

"Please, will you call me when you get to wherever you're going?"

When Faith didn't respond, Michael gazed up at Charles, his eyes swimming with tears. "I'll call you, Dad. Once we get there."

Faith started the car and reversed, and Charles watched his wife and son drive away, out of his life.

He sank to his knees on the hard pavement. That's where his strength would lie for this trial. Raising his gaze to the dark heavens, he cried out, "Oh God, help me. This is all my fault." He lowered his voice to a whisper. "Even Faith's indiscretion."

CHAPTER TEN

THE DRIVE to Cottonwood Falls had been long and tiring. Many times Faith had been tempted to pull in at a motel for the night, continue the journey the following day. But she'd pressed on, eager to get to her brother's house. It had helped that Michael was determined to stay awake to keep her company. She might not have made it more than halfway across Kansas if he hadn't.

Though sad and confused over what had transpired between her and his father, Michael was excited about the prospect of seeing his cousin again. Faith was grateful her son had that distraction at least. And Michael being with Charity would give Faith space to think about what she should do next.

It was almost five in the morning by the time they arrived at Brody's house. Her brother was up and waiting for them. Faith wasn't sure he'd actually gone to sleep, although he claimed to have set his alarm for four.

She and Michael tiptoed into the house after Brody, and he showed them to their rooms.

"You want some coffee?" Brody whispered as he set Faith's suitcase down beside her bed.

She shook her head. "If I have a cup, I'll never get to sleep. And I desperately need to sleep." In slumber she could shut her mind off from the events that had been the final tipping point of her world.

Brody gave her shoulders a sympathetic rub and stared at her. "All right. We'll talk in the morning. Or afternoon, whenever you wake up."

She offered him a weak smile. "We'll talk in the morning. I just need a few hours' shuteye."

After her brother left, Faith popped her head around Michael's door to say good night. He'd already passed out on top of his bed. Poor boy must have been exhausted, although he hadn't shown it once during their journey.

Faith opened the closet and pulled a light blanket from the top shelf. She covered Michael and kissed his forehead before turning out the light. She returned to her bed. And her thoughts. But the sleep Faith craved did not come easily.

She tossed and turned, her jumbled mind mimicking her body. Charles had cheated on her. Grayson did the very same thing so very long ago. She never thought she'd experience those feelings of utter failure as a woman ever again after Grayson's infidelity. Never thought she'd have to face this problem in her marriage. But suddenly, the past few years made sense. This Juliette with her long, dark hair and fuchsia pink lips had been the reason for Charles having grown distant. How long had their affair been going on? How long had Grayson's affair with Faibian's mother gone on before her pregnancy forced him to confess? Had it really been only that one-time mistake as he'd always claimed?

And Charles? Was it really not what she thought at all? Should she have given him the opportunity to explain himself? But if he had wanted to, he could have. It had taken Faith at least thirty minutes to pack. He could've said a lot in that time. Instead, he'd kept quiet.

One thing was certain: she would never trust a man again. Ever.

They were liars, and they were cheats.

The house echoed with emptiness. Charles hated it. And it had only been thirteen hours since Faith had left, taking Michael with her. Faced with the prospect of life without her, Charles had spent half the night on his knees, the other half tossing and turning in his bed. His very empty bed. He missed just knowing Faith was there beside him.

He poured himself a second cup of coffee and headed outside onto the deck, phone in his hand. Once he'd sat down in the morning sun, he tried Faith's number again. After several rings, it went to voicemail.

Again.

Where were his wife and son? Wherever they'd gone, had they arrived safely?

"Lord, please, let them be okay. And let the truth be known."

He still hadn't been able to raise Juliette on her phone either. If he could just talk to her, he'd be able to clear up this mess with Faith.

He hoped.

He prayed.

What would he do, though, if the truth was that he *had* cheated on Faith last night with Juliette? That lipstick on his collar was pretty damning evidence, trumpeting the fact that something had happened.

If he could only remember.

He'd call Becky. Maybe Faith had spent the night at her place. It would make sense since they were best friends.

He opened his contacts to B. Finding nothing, he scrolled down to R for Rebekah. Also empty. Darn, seemed he didn't have her number, unless it was listed under her surname, whatever that was now. Who could keep up with that woman's marriages?

There was only one other person he knew of who Faith might've contacted last night. Concern over his wife overruled the stupidity of what he was about to do.

Too much effort to go back inside to consult the yellow pages or to fire up his laptop to Google the information, Charles dialed 411.

Once he had the number he was looking for, his finger waivered over his cell phone before dialing.

"Screamin' Beans, good morning," a perky female voice shouted from the other side of the line, the loud background noise indicating a busy Saturday morning at the coffee shop.

"Morning. Is it possible to speak to the owner, Mr. Grayson Fuller?" Charles asked, his voice also raised.

"Let me see if I can find him. Who may I say is calling?"

"Charles Young. My wife is his son's math teacher."

The noise died down as the woman obviously cupped the phone. Seconds later, she said, "Please hold on, I'm transferring your call to Grayson's office."

"Charles," Grayson's voice boomed over the phone. "To what do I owe this pleasure?" Had to be sarcasm that dripped from his voice; couldn't be pleasantries. Why on earth would Grayson find it pleasurable to talk to him when the man was after his wife?

Didn't matter what he thought. He had to know.

"Grayson, have you heard from Faith—last night or this morning?"

"Nope. Haven't spoken to her since— Why?"

He'd changed the subject. How Charles would love to finish the sentence for him...*since you kissed my wife this Thursday.* Instead,

Charles opened his mouth to explain, then shut it. This was a stupid idea. He couldn't tell Grayson the reason he was looking for Faith was that she'd taken off into the night, that he hadn't heard from her in over twelve hours, that she wasn't answering her cell.

"It's nothing. Goodbye." Charles cut the call.

Even though he had hoped the man would have some news of Faith, he was relieved that he didn't. Disappointed, but relieved.

That only left Becky, and he didn't know how to contact her. Unless…

No, surely Faith wouldn't have been that reckless as to endanger her life and Michael's by driving through the night to her brother in Kansas. Nine hours on the road was a long time, especially when it was late and you were tired, hungry, and upset.

Stirring, Faith reached for her phone on the bedside table. She glanced at the time on the screen. Just after nine thirty—in the morning, she hoped. Groan, she should get up before she slept the entire day away.

The device vibrated in her hand, silently heralding an incoming call. She stared at the caller ID.

GF.

Grayson? Why was he calling? And how did he get her number? She hadn't given it to him.

She shimmied up in the bed and leaned her back against the padded leather headboard. She forced herself to wake up and answered. "Hello."

"Faith, are you all right?" Panic colored Grayson's voice.

"Grayson. How did you get my number?"

"From Becky, last week after you'd left the coffee shop. Are you okay?"

"Why wouldn't I be?" And why did he think something was

wrong?

Grayson exhaled a heavy breath. "Because I just had a call from your husband. He was looking for you. From the little we spoke, it seems that you went AWOL last night. Did something happen?"

How could she answer his question without answering it? If she said yes, she'd open herself up to further questions about why, which would lead to admitting to her ex-boyfriend that her husband had cheated on her. And based on the events of Thursday, Grayson would probably take that as a green light to further his own agenda. He had to have an agenda concerning her, didn't he? The man had admitted he was still in love with her, that he'd be there for her no matter what. Goodness, he'd thought of her when he'd named his son. Why wouldn't he want to swoop in and save her from a philandering husband?

"I'm fine. Just a sudden trip to my brother in Kansas."

That much was true. It had been sudden.

"And your husband doesn't know about it?"

"Of course he knows."

Grayson remained silent for a moment before speaking. "I'm sorry, I'm confused. Why did he ask then if I spoke to you last night or this morning?" He groaned audibly. "You don't think he knows about us, do you?"

"Grayson, there *is* no us. I love my husband. I've loved him far longer than I ever loved you. What we had...that was a long, long time ago."

"But the kiss on Thursday..."

"Initiated by you, not me."

"Yes, but you responded."

She had, albeit briefly. Did that make her as guilty as Charles?

In God's eyes, yes. *Marriage should be honored by all, and the marriage bed kept pure, for God will judge the adulterer and all the sexually immoral.*

While she may not have defiled their marriage bed as Charles had, Faith had allowed Grayson into her head. She'd been attracted to him—the way he looked at her, the things he said—and she'd foolishly allowed herself to remember the feelings they'd once shared. If she hadn't, she would never have kissed him back. He would have felt the sting of her hand against his cheek, not the softness of her lips responding to his.

"Grayson, I–I can't tutor Faibian outside of my classroom. I'm sorry. I'll find someone else for you and get them to call you."

"Faith, please don't do that. I need you."

"Goodbye, Grayson." She cut the call. Her finger hovered over her phone for a moment before she deleted his number.

Leaning her head back, Faith stared at the ceiling. Did Charles know? About her and Grayson's kiss? Surely he couldn't. But it would be foolish to rule out the possibility that someone had witnessed their kiss and told Charles. However, if he did know, why hadn't he used that information against her last night?

It didn't make sense.

Nothing made sense.

The door creaked open. "Mom, are you awake? Can I come in?"

"Of course, Michael." She dropped her phone between the bedcovers.

"Was that Dad you were talking to?"

She shook her head. "A friend."

Michael flopped down onto the bed beside her. "Have you spoken to Dad this morning?"

"No. Honestly, I just woke up."

"But you've spoken to a friend?" Questions burned in his blue eyes.

"They called me. Besides, you were the one who promised you'd let your Dad know where we were when we arrived." She patted the rumpled bedclothes to find her phone then handed it to

95

Michael. "You call him. Let him know we're at Uncle Brody's."

Michael took the device from her. Leaning forward, he kissed her cheek. "Thanks, Mom." He bounced off the bed.

"Close the door on your way out, Michael. I need to get dressed."

He swung around and frowned, looking so like his father. "You don't want to talk to Dad?"

"No." Especially not now. She had a lot of thinking to do before she felt she'd be ready to speak to Charles again.

The smell of freshly baked cinnamon rolls and brewed coffee drew Faith to the kitchen.

"Morning."

Charity dropped the hot tray onto the stove top. Hands covered with oven mitts, she rushed toward Faith and wrapped her arms around her. "Auntie Faith."

Faith hugged her niece tightly and sniffed the air. "Is that my recipe?"

Charity beamed. "Dad has me making them every Saturday morning since you taught me. Mom complains that I'm ruining her waistline." Her shoulders lifted in a shrug. "It's not like I'm holding a gun to her head and saying 'eat!'"

Faith chuckled.

"You want some coffee?" Charity had already segued across the floor to the coffee maker, gloves off. She dumped them on the counter beside the cups standing ready and lifted the carafe filled with a dark brew.

"I would love a cup." Faith glanced around the kitchen then turned her attention outside. She frowned. "Where is everyone?"

"Mom and Dad are in the studio gathering their canvases and paints for this afternoon. Michael went to call them."

"This afternoon?"

"Yeah. They're heading just outside of town to capture the late afternoon beauty of the wheat bales in the fields. They've a series of paintings commissioned. You'll have to ask them if you want more information though. That's about as much as I know." Charity slid a steaming cup over to Faith. A cinnamon roll filled the plate that followed.

Faith lifted the breakfast bun and took a bite. She chewed the sticky pastry, and then swallowed. "These are good. How are things?"

"Between my mom and dad?"

Faith nodded. Charity had confided in her when they'd recently visited. Since then, Faith had been concerned about her brother's marriage and had been praying for Brody, Madison, and Charity. Had marrying a woman eight years his junior come back to bite him?

"A little better. Still a bit rough at times—the arguments, the fights... I just keep praying for Mom and Dad, like you taught me. I think Dad's jealous of Mom's success. She seems to get more artwork commissioned than he does. Maybe that makes him feel like a failure...less like a man? I don't know."

"Well, maybe your dad needs to focus on what he's good at—running that art gallery—and leave the painting to your mom." Faith sipped her coffee.

"Maybe. But Dad does love being an artist too."

"Did I hear my name being taken in vain?" Brody strode into the kitchen, Madison and Michael following close behind.

Faith smiled at them as she set her cup down, her hands still wrapped around its warmth. "Charity was just telling me that you're planning on going out to paint this afternoon. Wheat bales?"

"We are. Unfortunately, the work was scheduled long before

you decided to come and visit." Brody poured himself and Madison a cup.

"I love wheat bales," Faith said softly to herself.

"How would my little sister like to come along and try her hand at painting a Kansas landscape?"

"Your little sister would love it."

Brody turned to Charity and Michael. "And you two? Feel like playing with paint today?"

Both their teen faces lit up.

"Seriously?" Michael's eyes widened. "As in our own pieces of art?"

"Uh-huh." Reaching for a cinnamon roll, Brody wrapped his fingers around the soft delicacy. He set his mug on the table then fell onto the stool beside Faith. "So what brings you all the way from the mountains to the prairies? Trouble in paradise?"

Faith slapped Brody's shoulder. "Can't I just visit my brother and his family on a whim?" Despite what had happened, she didn't want to smear Charles's name to her family.

Brody eyed her with suspicion. He leaned forward, closer to Faith, and whispered, "I could just ask my nephew."

Closing her eyes, Faith blew out a sigh before answering her brother. "Be my guest." Michael had promised to keep what had happened at home private.

A low chuckle rumbled from Brody. "I already did. He's not talking either."

Faith shrugged and took another swig of coffee. "Then maybe there's nothing to tell. Maybe we just wanted to visit, that's all."

"In the middle of the night? Ha, right." Brody finished his coffee and roll as they chitchatted before shoving to his feet. "I'll be in the studio if you want to talk."

As he strode away, Madison slid onto his seat. She placed her hand over Faith's. "If you ever need someone to confide in, I'm here."

And let her secrets fast become common knowledge in the Peterson households? Never. She'd rather call Becky.

CHAPTER ELEVEN

FAITH AND Michael had enjoyed their art lessons so much, they'd been eager to join Brody and Madison every day they went out to work on their sunset landscapes. Some days, Charity came with them. But today, Faith came alone. She was anxious to get her painting finished. She wasn't sure why. Maybe just for the reminder as the sun set that tomorrow it would rise again. That despite the deep heartache she felt right now, life went on. And it would for her too.

This was the fifth day in a row she was setting up her easel and canvas overlooking the hay bales in farmer Miller's recently cut fields. Today a big, red combine harvester was parked at the end of the field, and she considered adding it to the painting. Her artwork was coming along pretty well, if she had to say so herself. Not Peterson Studios standards, but definitely something she'd frame and hang up in her office back home.

Home... Where was that now? Where would it be in the future? Maybe she'd move back to Loveland, get a teaching job there. She'd always been happy in the smaller town. And it would be close enough for Charles to take Michael for weekends and holidays. She didn't want her son growing up with an absent father, as had been the case with Grayson and Faibian.

Her heart ached for Michael, caught in the middle of this mess, and her gaze misted. Swallowing back her tears, Faith squeezed more burnt umber and burnt sienna onto her pallet. She dabbed her brush into both oils and mixed a shade all her own, perfect for the edges of the dried bales and the furrows in the ground between the rows of harvested wheat.

She'd found the time out there in the fields, turning a bare canvas into something beautiful, extremely therapeutic. Maybe once she was settled, somewhere, she'd take up painting. Or pottery perhaps. That, too, must be healing...turning a gooey, ugly lump of clay into a useful and attractive vase.

Could God make something out of the shambles her life had become? Romans 8:28 said that in all things God works for the good of those who love him, who have been called according to his purpose. Did that...could that...include her broken marriage? This pot God held in His hands, the Young family, was marred. What would their family look like when He was done reshaping it?

Faith glanced at the time on her wristwatch. Seven. The sun would start setting in an hour, and dinner would probably be ready in as much time. She packed up her paints and easel and headed back to Brody and Madison's. Tomorrow she'd put the final touches to the piece, add in that harvester if it still stood in the field.

"I'm home," Faith shouted as she carefully carried her wet painting through the front door. She followed the passage through to Brody and Madison's studio and balanced her canvas on one of the empty easels to dry.

She spent a few minutes strolling around the studio, perusing the paintings of Kansas landscapes hanging there. Madison was so talented, Faith wished she could paint like her. Brody was also really good, but his wife had a definite edge on him in the finer details department. Her artworks held a depth that Brody hadn't quite mastered. She brought the beauty of Kansas to life.

Maybe Faith should move here instead of Loveland. Michael could be close to his only cousin. And Faith would have the support of her brother and sister-in-law. On weekends, they could teach her the various techniques and mediums for brushwork. Definitely an appealing option for life post Charles Young.

She'd pray about it. Maybe tomorrow, she'd open up to Brody. If she planned to move to Cottonwood Falls, she would have to tell her brother that her marriage was over, much as she hated to.

Faith had been so focused on getting her wet painting to the studio safely, that she hadn't noticed the delicious aromas wafting from the kitchen until she headed back that way. Both Brody and Madison hovered over the stove.

"Where are the kids?" Faith asked as she strolled into the kitchen.

"I think they're listening to music in Charity's room," Madison replied, holding out a spoon filled with a broth the color of her burnt umber and sienna mixture. "Taste this."

Faith filled her mouth with the liquid. She swallowed the warm broth then smacked her lips. "Ooh, yummy. That's delicious. What is it?"

Brody chuckled. "No idea. I threw in a little of this, and a little of that, and this is what I got. Not bad though."

"Not bad? It's amazing!" Faith pulled out one of the chairs around the kitchen table and sat. "Can I ask you a question? Two actually."

Both Brody and Madison nodded.

"Of course," Madison said as she began to set five places around the table.

"Why do you live in such a small town?"

Her brother and sister-in-law stared at each other for a moment.

Madison was the first to answer. "It's nice to be out of the bustle. And Emporia is only a half hour's drive away. When we go in to check on business and acquire stock for our gallery, we shop for anything we can't get here in Cottonwood Falls."

Brody stirred the contents in the large silver pot. "Artists are recluses, Faith, that's why."

At this point in her life, she wouldn't mind being a recluse.

"Do you like living in Cottonwood Falls?"

"We love it," Brody and Madison said in unison.

Faith couldn't stop herself from wondering whether she and Michael would love it too. She'd never lived anywhere other than in Colorado—Fort Collins, Denver, and Loveland. The thought of moving to another state both terrified and excited her.

Leaning back in his chair, Charles stared through the glass window of his office and watched his coworkers arriving. One by one they settled in behind their desks. Escaping the empty house, he had arrived at work way earlier than anyone else this week. He missed Faith so much, and she'd only been gone for five days. Why couldn't he have felt this way the last few years? Why had it taken losing her for him to realize just how much she really meant to him? How deep his feelings for her really were?

In hindsight, he recognized that he'd first had to make right with God—just as Jackson had intimated—before he could love his wife as Christ loves his bride, the church. Him. He would sacrifice anything to have Faith back in his life and in his arms.

Lord, what am I to do? How can I fix things with Faith? She won't take my calls.

Spotting Juliette heading toward her desk, his stomach lurched. He'd waited five long days for this moment. And now that it had arrived, he wanted to be anywhere except here. He wanted to be having a totally different conversation with his secretary than the imminent one he had to conduct.

She smiled and offered a quick wave as she set her handbag down beside her desk. She strode into his office. "Morning, boss." Like the tide creeping up the shore, her cheerful voice rippled toward him. The fact that he was about to dash her good mood did not feel great.

Charles straightened in his chair and leaned forward, crossing his arms on his desk. "Juliette, welcome back. How was your short vacation?"

"It was just great. I love the mountains, except for the fact that the cell phone signal there is the pits, or at least it is on my boyfriend's phone."

Boyfriend? He didn't realize she had one.

Juliette's breath hitched. "Speaking of phones, I saw a myriad of missed calls from you. I'm sorry, I accidentally left my phone at home. Only discovered I'd done that when we were halfway to Aspen. Wesley refused to go back for it. Anyway, we only got back late last night—I didn't want to call you then."

She reached for his arm and gave it a gentle squeeze before easing into the chair opposite him. "How are things? You're certainly looking a lot better than when I last saw you."

Lowering his gaze, Charles inhaled deeply. When he finally spoke, his voice held a tremor. "M–my wife left me."

"What? For that other guy?"

Charles shook his head. "It was my fault."

Tiny wrinkles formed on Juliette's forehead. "Your fault? I don't understand...unless you had an affair in retaliation." Her eyebrows peaked. "You didn't, did you?"

"I...don't know. I–I don't think so. I hope not." Charles rose from his chair. This was proving more difficult to talk about than he'd thought it would be, and way more awkward than it had been the times he'd replayed the scene in his head.

He strode across the office and closed the door before returning to his desk. But he didn't sit down. Instead, hands in his pockets, he turned his back to Juliette and gazed through the third-story window to the traffic bustling below.

"Faith found the note you left me at the hotel. I'd taken it with me with the intention of destroying it." He shrugged. "I forgot."

He bit the inside of his mouth lightly. "She also found the hotel receipt and a coaster from the bar. She knew I'd been lying about being at a conference in Denver."

"Didn't you tell her the truth? About seeing her with another man? About what their kiss did to you."

A low groan escaped Charles's throat. "I told you about that too?" He couldn't remember what all he'd said to Juliette that night.

"You did."

"I chose not to tell Faith. She found lipstick on my collar." Charles turned around slowly. "Your shade."

Placing his palms on his desk, he stared at her. "What happened after you took me to my hotel room? Did we—"

"No!" Shock reshaped her fine features. She sprang to her feet. "Of course not! How could you even think that?"

Straightening to her height, Charles replied, "Because you often said you'd do anything for me. I–I wasn't sure if *anything* included—"

"No!" Juliette took a step back. Reaching out, she placed a hand on the backrest of her chair. "You're a great boss, and an attractive man, and yes, I like to flirt, but I could never break up a marriage."

Charles breathed a relieved sigh as his neck heated. He sank into his seat and gestured for Juliette to do the same. "So how did the lipstick get on my collar?"

"You were quite drunk by the time I managed to get you upstairs to your room. You passed out and fell onto the mattress, dragging me with you. I landed on your shoulder. I–I guess that's how my lips managed to smudge your shirt. I'm really sorry. I was only trying to help."

"I know you were, Juliette. And it's not your fault. I don't blame you at all. So, what happened after that?" He hated pressing her, but he needed to get to the bottom of this; he needed all the facts before he could explain himself to Faith. "When I woke in the morning, my clothes were hanging on the chair. Did you—"

"I didn't undress you." By now, Juliette's expression was one of a woman on the verge of tears. "If you think that little of me, perhaps you need to find a new secretary."

"I'm sorry, Juliette. I don't want to lose you in the office, but I need answers."

She pursed her lips then gave an understanding nod. "I removed your shoes and placed them beside the desk. Then I covered you with a blanket and left. That's all."

The room had been too warm when he'd woken. Add to the fact that the air-conditioning had not been on, him being fully clothed, and a blanket on top of him as well, he must've stripped down and hung his clothes himself. Old habits did die hard. Pity he hadn't hung his clothes that night when he got home. But Faith had held onto his jacket, so she would likely still have found the coaster, although she probably wouldn't have looked any further if she hadn't seen that lipstick on his collar. Stupid. Why had he left his shirt on the bed? All he'd needed was a few days to find out from Juliette exactly what had happened, then he would have confessed to Faith, no matter what.

"I could call your wife and explain...tell her something had upset you that day. I don't need to go into details about what."

He shook his head. "Thanks for the offer, but it's my problem,

I'll take care of it."

Juliette nodded and headed for the door.

"One more thing," Charles called after her.

She paused and pivoted.

"Let's never speak of this again."

The relieved look on her face told Charles she was more than happy to comply with his request. Now if he could only get Faith to talk to him so that they, too, could speak of it once and then never again. If he didn't manage to contact her before the end of the day, he'd fly to Wichita from Denver after work tomorrow, then get a rental for the eighty-minute drive to Cottonwood Falls. Hopefully, Brody would welcome him into his home and he'd manage to convince Faith to return to Fort Collins with him.

Sadness washed over Faith as she dabbed the last stroke of red onto her canvas, completing not only the combine harvester she'd managed to add to her landscape, but her work of art too. She had loved losing herself between the pallet and her painting, leaving her troubles behind with every stroke of the brush. Should she start another one tomorrow, or return to the reality of her life and start making some important, life-changing decisions. So far, she hadn't received any direction from God. Once more, He remained silent.

The clock had just rolled past six thirty. She needed to get back to Brody and Madison's house. She'd promised them she'd cook dinner tonight.

Her thoughts turned to Charles. An hour behind Kansas time, he would be leaving the office around now, unless he was planning to work late. She couldn't help wondering about what he would make for dinner. Charles wasn't much good in the kitchen. He'd probably opt for a TV dinner heated in the microwave. Or would Juliette be prancing around Faith's kitchen preparing him a meal?

A more likely scenario was Charles and Juliette making the most out of their time without Faith around, and going out for romantic dinners every night.

Her cell phone rang and she shoved her hand in her jeans' pocket to tug it out. *Please don't let it be Charles again.* He'd tried calling her several times today, way more than he'd done on the other days since she'd left.

Faith stared at the unknown number on the screen, and her heart compressed as if someone had grasped it in their hand and tightened their fingers around it. What if something had happened to Charles?

She answered, "Hello, Faith Young speaking."

"Faith, please don't hang up the phone on me. I must speak with you. It's Juliette Johnson, your husband's secretary."

"Yes..." Faith's tone was devoid of warmth. The nerve of her calling. What could the woman possibly want?

"I promised Charles I wouldn't contact you, but I couldn't bear it when he left the office earlier and confirmed he still hadn't managed to get in touch with you today. Faith, you have to believe me when I tell you that there is nothing between Charles and me...never was, never will be."

"But—"

"Yes, the lipstick you saw on his collar was mine, but it didn't get there how you think it did."

Really... What lies have Charles and his secretary concocted?

"Well then, how did it get there?"

"Charles called me at the office last Thursday afternoon. He'd missed an important meeting. I had tried to contact him but his phone kept going to voicemail. He asked me to give his apologies and reschedule...that a family crisis had come up. Then he asked me to contact you and tell you he had to suddenly attend a conference in Denver." There was a pregnant pause before Juliette continued. "I'm so sorry I lied to you that day, but he sounded so angry. And upset."

Thursday. That was the day she'd had lunch with Grayson. The day he'd kissed her.

Juliette continued, "I offered Charles a listening ear if he needed it, and that's when he gave me the address of the hotel where he spent the night."

"With you…"

"No! By the time I got there, Charles had already drunk far too much."

Faith began to tremble. This was ludicrous. She should just cut this call. "Do you really expect me to believe that, Miss Johnson? My husband doesn't drink."

"Well he did that night," Juliette snapped back. "And I don't blame him one bit. Seeing his wife in the arms of another man…it's enough to—" She swallowed her words. "Oh gosh, I'm sorry. I shouldn't have said that."

"Excuse me?" Charles had seen Grayson kissing her? Why hadn't he said anything after she'd accused him of having an affair? He could have thrown that in her face, but he hadn't.

"Charles didn't want you to know he knew. I've no idea why."

"W–what happened when you found him at the hotel?" Faith's voice softened. Maybe she'd misread everything and accused her husband unjustly.

"He wanted another drink. I told the barman no more—only coffee. When Charles wanted an Irish, I threatened him with black coffee if he didn't behave. He'd already had far too many whiskeys."

Faith managed a small laugh. "He hates black coffee."

"I know. Anyway, he told me he'd blown things with you and forced you into another man's arms. Said he should have treated you better. I offered to drive him home, but he said he couldn't go home like that and reminded me that we had told you he was in Denver at a conference."

"He said all that?" Charles had realized that he hadn't been the husband he used to be? Why hadn't he just come to her the next day and told her?

"Yes. I booked him into the hotel for the night to sleep off his intoxication, then I helped him to his room. Soon as he saw the bed, he fell onto the mattress and passed out. But on the way down, he unintentionally dragged me with him. It was then that I face-planted him, leaving a trail of my lipstick on his collar. I'm sorry for all the pain this situation has caused you. I was only trying to help him."

"I understand." And Faith did. She had prayed that same night for God to protect Charles, and He had. What might her husband have done in his anger if he was sober? She might never have been able to restore her faith in him again.

But now…

"Juliette. Please don't tell Charles that you called me." She didn't want Juliette to get into more trouble. Poor woman felt responsible enough already.

Tomorrow was a new day, a clean canvas, and Faith had to choose what picture she and Charles would paint.

CHAPTER TWELVE

FAITH STOOD on her brother's back porch later that evening, gazing up into the night sky, contemplating the vastness of God as she studied the twinkling stars, their number beyond comprehension. And oh, how well she knew the concept of infinity. How could she hide from her own sin before an all-knowing, all-powerful, ever-present God?

She swiped at the tears that traced her cheeks. *Lord, I was at fault too. Please, forgive me.*

Behind her, a door creaked opened and shut.

"Mom, are you okay? You've been so quiet tonight."

"I'm fine, Michael." Faith sniffed and offered him a weak smile. She pulled him into a side hug. "Hey, I've some good news. We're going home tomorrow, so you'll need to pack your bag tonight."

Disappointment tugged his mouth down on one side. "Already? Charity and I still had so much planned. I–I thought we would be here a while longer."

He could stay. It would give her and Charles time alone, which they would probably need. They had a lot to work through.

"Would you like to stay? I could fly you home a few days before school starts."

Michael looked up at her, eyes bright. "Would you really let me stay longer?"

"Of course. I know how much you love spending time with your cousin."

"You're the best, Mom." Michael hugged her then turned to go.

"Um, Michael…don't say anything to anyone just yet. I still need to talk to Uncle Brody. All right?"

"My lips are sealed." He grinned and hurried back inside.

Faith sank onto the daybed swing. Rocking back and forth slowly, she closed her eyes and tried to imagine what she would do, what she would say when she saw Charles again tomorrow. If she left Cottonwood Falls around six a.m., she'd be back in Fort Collins by three that afternoon. She'd have enough time to freshen up and start dinner before Charles returned from work. Wouldn't he be surprised to see her there? She could only hope.

The swing lurched, and Faith started. Her eyes flew open to see Brody sitting beside her. She'd been so deep in thought she hadn't even heard the back door creak.

"Ope! Did I give you a fright?"

Faith smiled. She loved the way people in Kansas sometimes said oops. She shook her head in answer to her brother's question.

Brody stared at her. "So what's up, sis?"

Had she been that transparent tonight, failing to hide her scrambled thoughts? Ever since she'd spoken to Juliette and found out that Charles had seen Grayson kiss her and then chosen not to confront her, Faith's mind had spun like a hamster on a wheel. Round and round, faster and faster.

And the more she was confronted with her own sin, the more convinced she became that she heard God's voice speaking to her.

Restore faith.

Restore faith.

Restore faith.

Did He mean that she and Charles needed to restore their faith in each other, their faith in God, or that she needed restoration? Was God actually saying *restore Faith*?

She couldn't shake the feeling He meant all three of the above.

Placing her feet on the floor and her palms on the edge of the cushioned seat, Faith slowly turned to her brother. "Why?"

"You seemed...distracted tonight."

She nodded. "That's because I was."

"Anything you want to share?" He offered her a smile.

"I...um...I'll be returning to Fort Collins tomorrow. I need to get home. Michael wants to stay though. Would that be all right? Just another week or so. I'll fly him back home before school starts."

"Charity would like that. It would be good to have him here longer; he's a great kid."

"Thank you." Faith flashed a smile at Brody then looked away. She stared into the darkness of their backyard. "It's a beautiful night."

"It is. And those dark heavens where the stars seem to shine brighter are just one more reason we love staying out here." Brody sucked in a breath. "Can I ask you something?"

"Sure." Her head bobbed up and down with the single syllable.

"Is everything all right between you and Charles?"

Faith sighed. "They weren't...that's why I drove here so suddenly. But they will be. Soon as I get home. I've come to realize that it was all a big misunderstanding. Now I need to make things right again with Charles."

Brody pursed his lips, his chest rising and falling with each breath. "You know you'll always have a home here if things go wrong."

Clasping his hand in hers, she tightened her hold. "Thanks. That's good to know. But I have faith that everything will work out just fine." She patted her brother's leg then pushed to her feet. "I'd better pack if I'm to get an early start tomorrow."

"Goodbye!" Faith stuck her hand out the window and waved as she pulled away from her brother's house with little more in her car than herself and one lonely bag. Madison had promised to ship her artwork to her once the paint had finally dried.

As she didn't have Michael to keep her company, she turned on the radio. Faith envied her son flying back home. A nine hour road trip wasn't fun, especially on your own. But she was thankful to be making the return journey during the day. She'd been the one who had opted to take off across the country without thinking things through, so she had to take responsibility for the repercussions of her actions. And that meant a long drive back home. But despite that, being in Cottonwood Falls the past week had been food for her soul. She had no regrets about coming.

Many a time since last night, Faith had picked up her phone to call Charles. Then decided against it. This was something they had to talk about face-to-face, not discuss over a phone.

Faith veered off the I-70 in Hays to stretch her legs and grab a coffee to go, then again in Oakley for a quick and early lunch. She was eager to get home. Only another hour until she crossed the state line into Colorado. But those last three and a half hours on home state roads always seemed the longest, something akin to that last month of a pregnancy.

Her mind drifted to a happier time and place, almost fourteen years ago, when she'd found out she was expecting. She and Charles had decided to wait until the birth to find out the baby's sex. Charles was the proudest father ever; one would think he was the only man in the entire universe who had sired a son.

Reminiscing on their marriage during the road trip, Faith somehow gained clarity, able to see the cracks in their marriage more clearly. So often she hadn't been the wife she should have been. But the nights she'd turned away from Charles's affections, she'd been so tired. Running after a preschooler, teaching high school math, and maintaining a home all at the same time had been exhausting. Add to that trying to have a second child and not being able to get pregnant... That whole season of their lives had been mentally taxing. When they accepted the fact that Michael would probably be an only child, some of the pressure eased.

Despite those problems, they'd remained strong as a couple. Looking back though, Faith realized that she and Charles had really started to drift apart after they'd moved from Loveland to Fort Collins, when his job had demanded more of him.

What a difference fifteen miles had made.

Shortly past exit 336, Faith spotted a sign to Denver. Sixty more miles to the city. And then about the same to Fort Collins. She was finally on the home stretch. In her eagerness, her foot pressed heavier on the gas pedal. Noticing her speed, she eased the Subaru back to the limit of seventy-five miles per hour.

As she neared the outskirts of Denver, she kept a keen eye on the truck ahead of her. Soon as she got a gap, she would pass. Two cars whizzed by on the left. Faith checked the rearview mirror. The coast was clear. She moved into the left lane. As she did, the truck swerved, then braked. Smoke swirled into the air as large rubber tires scraped the asphalt. Faith slammed her foot on the brake pedal watching in horror as the truck jackknifed. The cab and trailer swiveled into a V. Faith's car careened toward the truck.

Hands gripping the steering wheel, she swung the car, trying to avoid the accident. The Subaru slid into a spin, and her world became a blurred merry-go-round ride, ending abruptly when her car flipped and rolled. And everything turned to black.

Charles was just about to walk into his two o'clock meeting in the boardroom when his cell phone rang. He didn't recognize the number. He paused to answer.

"Charles Young."

"Mr. Young? Mr. Charles Young?"

Isn't that what he'd just said? Tamping down his irritation, Charles answered, "Yes."

"This is Paramedic Baxter of the Aurora Fire Department, Station 5. Do you know a Faith Young? We found your number as the last person called on her cell phone."

Charles leaned against the wall for support as his legs weakened. "S–she's my wife. What's happened?"

"I'm sorry to tell you, Mr. Young, but there's been an accident on the I-70 just before the interchange to Denver International Airport. Your wife has been airlifted to Denver Health."

Airlifted?

"H–how is she?"

"Critical. She'll be going into surgery the moment she arrives. I'd advise you get to the hospital as soon as you can. And if you believe in God, pray."

"A–and my son?"

"Your son? Was he in the car too?"

"I–I don't know."

"We could have another one!" The paramedic shouted. "Mr. Young, here's my number. If you hear from your son, please contact me."

After giving Charles the number, the paramedic cut the call.

Charles ran to his office to get his car keys.

"Hey, where's the fire?" Juliette joked from behind her desk.

"There's been an accident. Faith...M–Michael..." Charles choked on the words. He shook his head. "I have to go."

Juliette shoved to her feet, eyes filled with concern. "Where?"

"Denver Health."

She followed after Charles as he ran toward the stairwell. "Is there anything I can do?"

"No. Yes... Call Jackson Moore. His number is in my Rolodex. Tell him to contact the church's prayer chain. Faith is in a critical condition, and at the moment, my son is missing."

As Charles hurried toward his car, he dialed Brody's number. *Please, pick up the phone.*

"Charles. This is a surprise," his brother-in-law said as he answered.

"Brody, were Faith and Michael on their way home today?"

"Faith, yes. Why?"

"And Michael?"

"No. He stayed on with us for a few more days. Faith said she'd fly him home before school started. Why?"

Charles broke down in tears. "Oh, thank God."

"Charles, what's going on?" Brody's voice held an edge of angst.

"It's Faith. T–there's been an accident. Near Denver. She's been airlifted to Denver Health. She's critical."

Please, Lord, don't let her die.

"What?" Brody breathed the word. "I–I'll fly to Denver with Michael. I'm sure there's a late afternoon flight from Wichita. We'll see you there. Do you want to speak to Michael?"

He'd love to. But he was too scared. What if Michael blamed Charles for Faith's accident?

"I–I need to make more calls, Brody. Will you let him know? Please. And tell him...tell him that I love him."

"I will."

"Thank you. Please, take care of my son."

"See you later, Charles." Brody cut the call.

Charles hopped into his SUV and started the engine. Before driving off, he dialed the paramedic's number and informed him that Michael was safe, that he hadn't been inside the car with his mother.

And then he prayed for Faith, leaving his wife's fate in the hands of the doctors and her Creator.

Faith was still in surgery by the time Charles arrived at Denver Health, little more than an hour after he'd received the news. He took a seat in the surgical waiting room where the inquiry desk had advised him to wait for news.

Faith had been in the OR for probably close on three and a half hours when a nurse approached.

"Mr. Young?"

Charles shoved to his feet. "Yes… My wife?"

"I'm nurse Bennett. Dr. Evans requested that I update you on your wife's condition. She has suffered severe injuries—a fractured knee, internal bleeding, and a traumatic brain injury. But an excellent team of doctors are working on her and doing everything they can to save her."

"H–how much longer will she be in surgery?"

"At least another two hours." The nurse rested a comforting hand on Charles's arm. "There's an interfaith chapel on the second floor of Pavilion B if you need a quiet place to wait. We can arrange for a chaplain to pray with you, if you'd like."

Charles nodded and swallowed hard. "Thank you. I'll ask at the front desk if I need someone. Just do whatever's necessary to save my wife. Please."

"We will. Have faith."

As the nurse walked away, Charles took the stairs to the second floor. Time spent in prayer in the chapel was what he needed. As did Faith. The doctors were doing what they could—he had to do what was in his power to do. And that was pray.

Give me a chance to make things up to her, please, Father.

His soul spent of prayers, Charles made his way back to the waiting area from the chapel. He stopped at the coffee shop for a hot cup, glancing at his watch as he entered the café. Seven p.m.? Had he really prayed for over an hour?

He paused at the counter. Having had a change of mind, he ordered his coffee to go. Brody and Michael had caught a late afternoon flight to Denver and would be arriving soon. He needed to get back to the waiting room.

Charles detoured past the inquiry desk. He cleared his throat. "Excuse me, but has there been any news on Mrs. Faith Young? She's in surgery with a Dr. Evans."

The young woman typed on her keyboard then looked up at Charles. "I'm sorry, but she's still in surgery."

"Thank you." He'd so hoped she would be out and that he could see her.

Charles slid into a chair and took a long drink from his Styrofoam cup, eyeing the guy sitting opposite him a few seats down. What the—? Of all the nerve. What was *he* doing here?

Charles set his cup down on the floor beside his chair before rising. He strode across to Grayson. "What are you doing here?" Rage inflamed his tone.

Grayson shot to his feet, extending a hand.

Charles ignored it.

"I–I heard about Faith's accident."

"How?"

"My son, Faibian." Grayson pointed to the good-looking young man sitting beside him. "Your church's prayer chain extended to Faith's students. We came as soon as we heard."

The boy stood. He tipped his head. "I'm sorry about Mrs. Young. She's a good teacher. I hope she gets well soon."

Forgetting how much bigger Faith's ex-boyfriend was than him, Charles gripped Grayson on the upper arm and tugged him a few steps away. "You shouldn't be here. You've no right—"

"I have every right. You don't love her. I do."

"How dare you?" Charles's hand curled into a tight ball and before he could even think, his fist connected with Grayson's chin.

Grayson staggered back and dropped to the floor. "Are you crazy?" He rubbed his jaw.

Faibian rushed to his father's side and fell to his knees. "Dad! Are you okay?" The boy's heated gaze met Charles's.

Charles wouldn't back down. He pointed at his rival. "You need to go home."

"And if I don't?" Grayson challenged.

"Then I'll make you." Charles leaned over and gripped Grayson's T-shirt at the neck. "Stay. Away. From. My. Wife."

"Dad! No! What are you doing?"

Michael?

Oh no, what all had his son witnessed?

Releasing Grayson, Charles pivoted and rushed to his family. He swept Michael into his arms with a fresh flood of tears. "Son, I'm so glad you're okay."

"Where's Mom? Can we see her yet? How is she?"

Charles's tears turned to shaky sobs at the uncertainty of Faith's condition. He held on tight to Michael, struggling to regain his composure. "S–she's in a bad way. She should be out of surgery shortly. I'm sure the doctor will be along soon to update us."

Brody bear hugged Charles then walked over to where Faibian

had helped his father to his feet.

"Grayson Fuller, it's been a lifetime, but things make a whole lot of sense now." He leaned in closer to Grayson. "A word of advice... Stay away from my sister."

CHAPTER THIRTEEN

"SHE'S COMING around. Page Dr. Evans. And call her husband."

Who was that speaking?

Faith groaned and tried once again to open her eyes to see who the voice belonged to. Someone dressed in white hovered around her...bed? Where was she? *Am. I. Dead?* She failed to vocalize the three small words. Beside her, something whooshed but her eyes were too heavy to try and see where the cacophony of sounds was coming from—a rackety engine mixed with a loud, steady heartbeat mixed with the blustering suction of air. Like a slow waltz the noise repeated...one, two, three...one, two, three. Suck, beat, beat. Suck, beat, beat. Afraid, a tear leaked down her cheek and she swallowed. Her throat hurt.

"Faith, can you hear me?" A man's voice this time, not one she recognized. He opened one of her eyes and shone a small light into it—this way, then that—repeating the action with the other.

She tried to nod, but the movement hurt her head. In fact, her entire body ached, like she'd been hit by a bus.

An image of a white cab and trailer filling the road at an awkward angle, coming closer and closer, engulfed her mind as the tsunami of reality crashed her world.

"I'm Dr. Evans. You were in an accident. You're at Denver Health in surgical intensive care. You've been in a medically induced coma for the past five days."

Five days?

Michael... Was he in the accident too? If only she could talk. She whimpered.

"You're all right, Faith. You're going to be all right. Your husband and son are waiting outside the room. Are you up to seeing them for a short while?"

A gentle wave of relief washed over her as she tried once again to nod. And smile. Difficult with something shoved down your throat and your mouth taped shut.

"We'll start weaning you off the ventilator this afternoon. Once we're satisfied that you can breathe on your own, the breathing tube will be removed."

Her doctor had a soft voice. She liked him. Had he saved her life?

"Mom!"

"Faith..."

Her heart beat faster at the sound of Charles and Michael's voices. She hadn't spoken to Charles since that awful night. What would she say? Well, nothing at this time...but soon enough she'd be able to talk.

"Come on in," her doctor said. "Look who's awake." Faith could hear the smile in his voice. "We started reducing the dosage of pentobarbital last night, and these guys have been patiently waiting all day for you to come out of your coma."

Charles and Michael came closer to the bed and their faces became less blurred. Faith blinked slowly, trying to focus.

Michael reached for her and lightly touched her shoulder, as if he was afraid she'd break if he got too close. She nuzzled her cheek against his fingers and his shoulders shook as he began to weep.

Charles stood beside Michael. He gently took her hand between both his latex-gloved hands. "Thank God you're alive." Was he crying too?

Her eyes heavy, Faith closed them, and time seemed to drift away. She woke with a start and someone touching her foot. Michael no longer stood beside her. Charles had moved into the spot she'd last seen her son. She held his gaze, questioning her husband with her eyes.

"Michael stepped out to let Brody see you. ICU visitor rules."

She turned her attention away from Charles to the bottom of her bed.

Brody? Her brother was here too?

"Hey, sis." He wiped his cheeks and smiled at her. "T–Tyler sends his love. He wanted to be here, but couldn't leave Hope alone at home."

Faith slowly shifted her gaze back to her husband. Everything within her fought to be free of the machines and tubes attached to her body. She wanted to talk to Charles, to ask for his forgiveness and tell him she forgave him too. She wanted to kiss him, to whisper that she loved him and let him know how grateful she was that God had spared her to live more days on this earth with him and their son.

Scripture filled her mind, dissipating her frustration. Romans 12 verse 12. *Be joyful in hope, patient in affliction, faithful in prayer.* And then 1 Corinthians 13 verse 4. *Love is patient, love is kind.* She would be joyful and patient and kind in her affliction. Maybe God wanted her silent for this time so that she could be faithful in praying for her marriage and her husband. They would get their time to speak. Soon.

Excitement welled in Faith's belly. Today she would leave the cocoon of the intensive care unit and be moved to general surgery. Ten days had passed since the accident. Ten days she'd been carefully monitored, twenty-four seven.

She and Charles had still not been able to speak. No time alone. Michael was always with him and visiting hours in ICU were strict and limited. On top of that, her voice was still weak, hoarse from the intubation, but the speech therapy she'd been receiving the past three days had been helpful.

Dr. Evans was extremely pleased with her progress, although he warned that months of physical therapy lie ahead to strengthen her damaged knee. He also told her she might walk with a slight limp for the rest of her life. Would her students mock her behind her back? Should she even think about returning to teaching? It would be months before she'd be ready to go back to the classroom.

Her doctor had said she was a walking miracle—okay, maybe not walking, yet, but that would come—and that they hadn't expected her to pull through when she'd been brought into the emergency room that fateful Friday afternoon. Thankfully, nobody else had been hurt in the accident. The police said if her car hadn't flipped and rolled off the highway, she would have smashed into the jackknifed truck and more than likely been killed on impact.

God was good. Even in the darkness, He was good.

The trucking company had taken responsibility for the accident—driver negligence...he'd been talking on his cell phone—and would compensate Faith for her medical bills, loss of income, and a whole bunch of other legalese she didn't understand when Charles had explained it to her yesterday.

"Morning, Faith," Dr. Evans greeted cheerfully as he came to stand beside her bed. "They'll be moving you soon. I just wanted to do some final tests." He held up two fingers. "How many fingers do you see?"

She smiled and answered in a soft voice, not whispered because her speech therapist had advised against whispering, "Two."

"And what is one plus one?"

"Two."

"And five minus three?"

"Two." She chuckled. "What is this? Mathematics for dummies? You do know I have my degree in math. Instead, why don't you ask me to calculate the hypotenuse of a triangle or to solve a linear equation?"

He burst out laughing. "You know what? I think you're almost ready to go home, young lady."

"Is that young with a small or capitalized 'Y'?" Faith smiled and raised a questioning brow.

Faith was moved to a cozy two-bed ward with a private bathroom. Nobody occupied the other bed, and Faith didn't mind one bit. Trying to conserve her voice by speaking softly without whispering, she wouldn't be good company at the moment anyway. And she didn't need some chatterbox on the verge of going home as a roommate.

The physical therapist, who introduced herself as Sharon, came to see Faith shortly after her transfer. First thing she did was get Faith out of bed for a walk. Even though aided by crutches, it had been slow going. Still, Faith managed to get to the bathroom and back to her bed—about the same distance as from her bed to her own en suite bathroom back home. It had felt good to use the toilet again and not a bedpan.

Sharon helped Faith through a few muscle-strengthening exercises before tucking her back into bed.

"Do you think I could have a shower tomorrow? Give up the bed baths?" Faith reached for the glass of water standing on the bedside cabinet. She took a long sip through the straw. She needed to keep her vocal cords well hydrated.

"Maybe not tomorrow," Sharon said, "but definitely in a few days. Once you're a little stronger and steadier."

There was a soft knock on the door. Charles entered bearing a large bouquet of red roses in a crystal vase and a wide smile. Faith hadn't been permitted flowers in ICU. "Look at you. You ready to come home?"

"I wish." Faith couldn't help but wonder if Charles found her soft, breathy voice attractive. At least the bruising on her body and face had started to fade to a yellow and brown. They'd barely be noticeable soon. The scars on her body...they would last a lifetime. It was up to her to make certain the scars on her soul didn't.

"I'll see you later this afternoon, Faith. Physical therapy twice a day." Sharon waved and stepped out of the ward.

Charles set the vase down on the cabinet and pulled up a chair beside Faith's bed. He leaned over and kissed her before sitting. "How are you feeling?"

"Stronger every day. Where's Michael?"

Charles took her hand in his. "He's at Jeremy's house. I asked him to stay today. I hope you don't mind. I thought we could talk. We need to talk."

Faith offered Charles a weak smile. "We do. It's ten days overdue."

"Ten days?" A frown wrinkled his brow.

"I was on my way home to you, when the accident happened. I was so close. I'm sorry."

He smoothed his thumb over her skin. "Hey, it's not your fault. I'm just so unbelievably thankful that you pulled through."

"No, I'm sorry I didn't stay that night and listen to your

127

explanation. I shouldn't have taken off without knowing the full story."

Charles cocked his head to one side. "And…you know the full story…now?"

"Yes. I do." Of course, he didn't know that she knew. She'd told Juliette not to say anything. "Please, don't get angry with Juliette, but she called me the day before I left Kansas. She told me everything."

Tears began to trickle down Faith's cheeks. "Why didn't you tell me what you'd seen?"

He shook his head. "The morning after I'd gotten so drunk, I drove to Loveland and wandered around. Then I went to the mountains. As I strolled down memory lane, I fell in love with you again. And up in the mountains, I fell back in love with God. I made Him a promise that I wouldn't raise the subject of Grayson and his kiss, unless you did."

"You could have thrown that in my face as your defense. But you didn't. Why?"

Lifting Faith's hand, Charles pressed it to his lips, his blue eyes brimming. "That wouldn't be forgiveness, now would it?"

"I need you to know that nothing happened with Grayson beyond that one momentary kiss. Even so, it was wrong. Can you ever forgive me?"

Charles's mouth curved. "My darling, Faith. Everything has already been forgiven."

Faith lowered her gaze. "He made me feel special and loved at a time when I felt unloved and lonely. I'm so sorry I allowed myself to be swept away in the moment."

"It's not your fault. I treated you so badly, and I'm sorry. Please, forgive me."

"I forgive you," Faith said softly as she held Charles's gaze.

Charles wiped the moisture from his cheeks. "It has been my

prayer that as we talk things through and rebuild our trust in each other, that we'll discover all the things we did wrong so that we never make the same mistakes again."

"I would like that. I know I did many things too, by omission or commission, that added to the slow decline of our marriage." Faith's own tears flowed freely now. "I love you, Charles. I always will."

"I love you too. I promise to remain faithful to you—in mind, body, and soul—and to God, for as long as I live." He rose and kissed her ever so gently.

She smiled up at him. "I won't break, Charles. I'm stronger than you realize."

So he deepened the kiss. No more need for words, and Faith was glad. Her speech therapist's orders were that she take a thirty-minute break from speaking if her throat hurt. The therapist had said nothing about other activities involving the lips.

Unable to fall asleep again after the early morning rounds of the nursing staff, Faith limped to the bathroom on her crutches. She huffed, then limped back to her bed and grabbed the clothes Charles and Michael had brought her yesterday from the cabinet beside her bed, along with her toiletry bag. A lengthy, hot shower might ease her frustration at still being in Denver Health for yet another day. If only Dr. Evans had discharged her yesterday, she could've been home to see Michael start a new school year. But the doctor had been away for the weekend, and had said he'd only make a decision this week about her going home. So she would shower and get dressed in the hope that he would discharge her today. Soon as she knew, she'd call Charles to fetch her. She was so tired of being in the hospital. After sixteen days, she was more than ready to go home.

Becky had visited twice last week, and although her visits hadn't been long, Faith had enjoyed seeing her friend again. And, Becky had brought coffee, the drinkable kind.

Faith turned on the tap and waited until the shower rained warmth. Holding onto the rails, she carefully stepped under the water. She squeezed some shampoo into her palm then smoothed her hands over her wet hair. As she worked the lather between her fingers, the short hair at the base of her neck pricked her skin. Fortunately, the rest of her long hair hid the fact that part of her skull had been shaved for surgery.

She rinsed her hair until the water ran clear. Her gaze followed the droplets trailing her skin, down her shoulder and past the scar that ran from between her breasts to halfway down her stomach. She eased her left leg forward and turned her attention to the vertical cut across the knee. As she stared at the bright red lines that marred her body, she promised herself that her scars would not remind her of the accident. Rather, she determined they'd serve as a reminder of the consequences of not being open and honest. If only she had asked Charles to explain the night she thought she'd uncovered his "affair." If only she'd been brave enough to admit to her own failures and begged for her husband's forgiveness. If only she'd done many things, she would never have gone to Kansas— not that she regretted the healing being there had brought to her soul. She never wanted her scars to have been in vain.

Openness and honesty, that's what she and Charles had pledged to each other going forward.

Back in her bed, dressed in loose cotton slacks and a matching sleeveless blouse in a soft minty green, Faith dried her hair then put on some makeup. It felt good to pamper herself again.

She glanced at the door for the umpteenth time. Where was her doctor? When would he finally get around to seeing her? Discharging her?

After eating the breakfast that had arrived while she was doing her makeup, Faith grabbed her Bible from the cabinet drawer. She would have her quiet time while she waited.

Faith was deep into Psalm 139 when she heard a knock. She lowered the Bible onto the bedspread and looked up. The person entering was hidden behind the biggest bouquet of red roses. Her heart skipped a beat. Was her husband *that* happy she was coming home? But why would he bring flowers all the way to the hospital just to take them back home again? And why hadn't he waited for her call? Nothing was set in stone that she'd be discharged today.

"Morning, beautiful." Grayson peeked out from behind the bouquet before setting the vase of flowers down on the overbed table.

"Grayson, what are you doing here?"

"I needed to see how you were doing. I came the day of the accident, but..." He shifted on his feet then shoved his hands into his jeans' pockets. He lowered his gaze to the floor. "Both your husband and brother warned me to stay away."

Her heart warmed at the thought of Charles and Brody being so protective over her.

Grayson looked up at Faith and moved closer. "I've been getting updates on your condition from Becky. I suspected Charles wouldn't be here yet with school starting, so I came as early as visiting hours permitted."

He certainly had. She'd barely eaten breakfast.

"Did Becky tell you to come this morning?" She'd have to have a word with her friend if she had.

"No. I just figured he wouldn't be here until later." He reached for her hand, but she pulled away.

"You shouldn't be here, Grayson. I have nothing to offer you." Not even friendship. She'd skirted around being friends and look where that had gotten her.

"I meant it when I said I'm still in love with you, Faith."

She held his gaze. "And I meant it when I told you that I love my husband."

"Are you still apart? You left him, didn't you? That's why you were in Kansas, wasn't it?"

"We're only apart because of this hospital separating us. That's all."

Faith's cell phone rang, moving on the wooden surface of the bedside cabinet with each buzz. Faith reached for it and answered the call. "Hi honey."

"Morning, my darling. How are you feeling today?"

"Ready and raring to go home."

"Has Dr. Evans been?"

"Not yet, but I'm sure any minute now he'll be doing his rounds." Faith tried to ignore the fact that Grayson was in the room, but as soon as she saw Charles, she would tell him of Grayson's visit. Openness and honesty, all the time, no matter what.

"Well, I'm going to preempt Dr. Evans and his decision. I'm on my way. I'll see you in about thirty minutes."

"I can't wait." Faith flashed a look at Grayson before settling her gaze on her Bible lying on the bed in front of her. "I love you, Charles. Drive safely."

She cut the call then exchanged the phone for the Bible. She smoothed her hand across its black, leather covering. "I live by this book. And I know you did once upon a time too. I'm sure you remember what it says about another man's wife."

"I'm not…"

Faith stared into Grayson's eyes. "Forget about me, make right with God and then find yourself someone to spend the rest of your life with. Faibian's mother would be a wise place to start first. Your son deserves a full-time father."

"Faith, wait—"

"Goodbye, Grayson. You do need to go now. I hear my doctor's voice in the corridor. Thank you for stopping by to see how I'm doing."

Grayson turned and walked away. Pausing at the door, he looked back at Faith. "I will always love you."

"Then I pity you, because I cannot return that love." She reached for the call button and pressed it.

Moments later a nurse eased past Grayson, still rooted in the doorway. "I'm so sorry, sir." She hurried toward Faith. "You called, Mrs. Young? Is everything all right?"

"Yes, everything's fine. I just wanted to give you these beautiful roses to place at the nurses station for the staff to enjoy. You've all done so much for me."

"Certainly. Thank you, Mrs. Young." The nurse lifted the vase from where Grayson had set it down minutes earlier. "Are you going home today?"

Faith smiled at her before glancing toward the empty doorway. "I hope so. I have faith that I will."

EPILOGUE

Thursday, June 3, 2004

A STRANGE sense of déjà vu swept over Faith as she drew on the chalkboard. She turned to her class. "And that is how you do a linear equation."

No books slammed closed this time. No dark-eyed, hauntingly familiar, eleventh graders stared back at her.

Faith often wondered how Faibian had fared this last year of his schooling. She hoped he'd done well. The teacher who had taken over from her when the school year had begun way back in September, apparently came with a great resume. At least according to the school's principal.

Mr. Turnbill had been sad to lose Faith as a teacher, but with the months of physical therapy that had lain ahead, there was no way she could continue teaching. Besides, the end of her career at Colorado High had been inevitable. By Christmas, Charles had secured a job at a new accounting firm in Loveland. And before Valentine's, they'd moved into a beautiful new home in the town that held so many wonderful memories for them.

A bell rang and students started shoving to their feet.

"Wait," Faith said, smiling. "Have a wonderful summer vacation, everyone. Stay safe, don't do anything stupid, and I'll see you in September." She hoped.

"Bye, Mrs. Young," they sang together before rushing for the door.

She would miss her students, even though she'd only been teaching at Loveland High for the past six weeks. Already, her students had come to hold a special place in her heart. So she would continue to pray that a permanent opening would become available. Maybe the teacher she'd temporarily replaced would choose not to return.

Faith packed her teaching materials into her briefcase, then headed for her car, her limp not nearly as noticeable as it had been at the beginning of the year.

Michael was waiting for her when she got to the Lexus. When the insurance paid out for her vehicle, Charles had suggested she get a car like his, the only difference being the white color and that he'd insisted she now drive an automatic.

They slipped onto the leather seats.

"So, are you excited, Michael?"

"Two weeks in a mountain cabin with you and Dad? You bet!" A wide grin filled Michael's face.

By the time they got home, Charles was already waiting eagerly, his SUV packed. He helped Faith out of her car, then wrapped her in his embrace, greeting her with a long kiss. "You ready to go?"

She nodded. "Almost. I just need to change into something a bit more casual and then we can leave."

"I packed lunch for us. We can eat on the way."

"You did? I'm impressed. Since when did you get so domesticated, Mr. Young?"

A deep laugh rumbled and spilled from his lips. "Your accident did far more than just bring us back together, sweetheart. Look at me, I'm practically Mr. Mom. Who would have guessed?"

Who would have? God certainly did have a sense of humor. With Faith in the hospital for so long and then having to take it easy after she returned home, Charles had quickly learned to do so many things around the house—he'd found where the vacuum cleaner lived, how the iron and dishwasher worked, and which recipes in her cookbook were user-friendly. He'd proven himself a worthy candidate for home executive. And although she wasn't ready to hand over the reins of her kitchen, she did enjoy having her husband at her side as they prepared meals...just like she'd seen Brody and Madison do.

Faith changed into her favorite cotton dress, perfect for the warm June weather, and a pair of flat, white sandals to match. She smiled as Charles entered their room. "How do I look?"

"Like a beautiful angel," he said, embracing her. "You ready?"

"Yep."

They hurried to the car. Michael had already made himself comfortable on the backseat and tucked into the lunch box. "Come on, Mom and Dad, let's go."

"Yes, let's." Faith was as eager to see where Charles had booked as their son was to leave.

Nothing but forests and mountains surrounded the rustic, two-bedroom, wooden cabin with a loft, tucked away in the Wild Basin Area of the Rockies. Faith strolled out onto the large, raised wooden deck. She sighed, taking in the beauty around them.

"Charles, this place is amazing."

Charles drew her into his arms and whispered in her ear, "No, you are amazing. I love you with all my heart, Mrs. Young."

"And I you." Their lips met and butterflies took flight in Faith's belly. This was almost like being on their honeymoon again…just better. They'd been through the fire and come out stronger.

She took Charles's hand. "You want to go for a walk?"

"Are you up to it? Your leg…"

"Honey, I won't break, as long as you're there beside me to hold my hand and make sure I don't stumble and fall. Besides, my physical therapist said walking is good for the healing process."

"All right." He turned toward the house and shouted, "Michael, you want to come with us? Your mother and I are going for a walk."

Michael skidded out onto the deck. "For sure!"

Faith and Charles strolled hand in hand on the path dwarfed by towering pine trees, while Michael skipped on ahead.

"Mom! Dad! You gotta see this," Michael shouted from up ahead.

They tried to pick up the pace. Soon they arrived at the clearing where Michael stood gazing at the mountains ahead.

Charles stepped beside him and placed a hand on his shoulder. He pointed to the left. "That gray mountain over there is Mt. Meeker. The one farther back is Longs Peak, and beside that, Mt. Lady Washington."

"What a stunning view." Faith opened her arms and twirled around. "I feel like I'm on top of the world."

She had never felt so alive before. God had restored her, He'd restored her husband, and He'd restored their marriage. But most of all, He had restored their faith.

She closed her eyes, feeling the warmth of the sun on her face, and breathed a prayer to heaven. "Thank you, Jesus."

THE END

GLOSSARY

FoCo : Short for Fort Collins

Ope : [exclamation – Midwest slang] Sometimes used to show recognition of a mistake or minor accident, often as part of an apology

Rolodex : [Trademark] A small desktop file containing cards for names, addresses, and phone numbers

I hope you enjoyed reading *Restoring Faith*. If you did, please consider leaving a short review on Amazon, Goodreads, or Bookbub. Positive reviews and word-of-mouth recommendations count as they honor an author and help other readers to find quality Christian fiction to read.

Thank you so much!

If you enjoyed this book, you might like to read the other two books in this series, *Recovering Hope* (Shaped by Love - Book 2) and *Reclaiming Charity* (Shaped by Love - Book 3).

See The Potter's House Books for more details, http://pottershousebooks.com/

 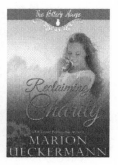

If you'd like to receive information on new releases, cover reveals, and writing news, please sign up for my newsletter.

http://www.marionueckermann.net/subscribe/

ABOUT MARION UECKERMANN

A Novel place to Fall in love

USA Today bestselling author MARION UECKERMANN's passion for writing was sparked when she moved to Ireland with her family. Her love of travel has influenced her contemporary inspirational romances set in novel places. Marion and her husband again live in South Africa and are setting their sights on retirement when they can join their family in the beautiful Cape.

Please visit Marion's website for more of her books:
www.marionueckermann.net

You can also find Marion on social media:
Facebook : Marion.C.Ueckermann
Twitter : ueckie
Goodreads : 5342167.Marion_Ueckermann
Pinterest : ueckie
Bookbub : authors/marion-ueckermann
Amazon : Marion-Ueckermann/e/B00KBYLU7C

TITLES BY MARION UECKERMANN

CONTEMPORARY CHRISTIAN ROMANCE

CHAPEL COVE ROMANCES
Remember Me *(Book 1)*
Choose Me *(Book 4)*
Accept Me *(Book 8)*
Trust Me *(Book 10)*
Releasing 2020
Other books in this tri-author series are by
Alexa Verde and Autumn Macarthur

THE POTTER'S HOUSE
Restoring Faith *(Shaped by Love - Book 1)*
Recovering Hope *(Shaped by Love - Book 2)*
Reclaiming Charity *(Shaped by Love - Book 3)*

A TUSCAN LEGACY
That's Amore *(Book 1)*
Ti Amo *(Book 4)*
Other books in this multi-author series are by: Elizabeth Maddrey, Alexa Verde, Clare
Revell, Heather Gray, Narelle Atkins, and Autumn Macarthur

UNDER THE SUN
SEASONS OF CHANGE
A Time to Laugh *(Book 1)*
A Time to Love *(Book 2)*
A Time to Push Daisies *(Book 3)*

HEART OF ENGLAND
SEVEN SUITORS FOR SEVEN SISTERS
A Match for Magnolia *(Book 1)*
A Romance for Rose *(Book 2)*
A Hero for Heather *(Book 3)*
A Husband for Holly *(Book 4)*
A Courtship for Clover *(Book 5)*
A Proposal for Poppy *(Book 6 - Releasing 2020)*
A Love for Lily *(Book 7 - Releasing 2021)*

HEART OF AFRICA
Orphaned Hearts
The Other You

HEART OF IRELAND
Spring's Promise

HEART OF AUSTRALIA
Melbourne Memories

HEART OF CHRISTMAS
Poles Apart
Ginger & Brad's House

PASSPORT TO ROMANCE
Helsinki Sunrise
Soloppgang i Helsinki
(Norwegian translation of Helsinki Sunrise)
Oslo Overtures
Glasgow Grace

ACFW WRITERS ON THE STORM
SHORT STORY CONTEST WINNERS ANTHOLOGY
Dancing Up A Storm ~ *Dancing In The Rain*

NON-FICTION
Bush Tails
(Humorous & True Short Story Trophies of my Bushveld Escapades
as told by Percival Robert Morrison)

POETRY

Glimpses Through Poetry
[Bumper paperback of the four e-book poetry collections below]

GLIMPSES THROUGH POETRY
My Father's Hand
My Savior's Touch
My Colorful Life

WORDS RIPE FOR THE PICKING
Fruit of the Rhyme

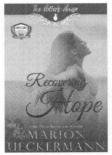

In a single moment, a dream dies, and hope is lost.

Lovers of the ocean, Hope and Tyler Peterson long for the day they can dip their little one's feet into its clear blue waters and pass on their passion for the sea.

Despite dedicating her life to the rescue and rehabilitation of God's sea creatures, when their dream dies, Hope can't muster the strength to do the same for herself. Give her a dark hole to hide away from the world and she'd be happy…if happiness were ever again within her reach.

While Tyler is able to design technology that probes the mysteries of the deep, he's at a loss to find a way to help Hope surface from the darkness that has dragged her into its abyss. He struggles to plan for their future when his wife can barely cope with the here and now.

If they can't recover hope, their marriage won't survive.

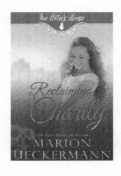

Some artworks appear chaotic, but it all depends on the eye of the beholder.

Brody and Madison Peterson have the picture-perfect marriage. Or so it seems. But their teenage daughter Charity knows only too well that that's not the case. Frequent emotive arguments—the bane of artistic temperaments—have Charity pouring out her heartache and fears in her prayer journal.

When Madison makes a career choice that doesn't fit in with her husband's plans for their lives or their art gallery, disaster looms. The end of their marriage and a bitter battle over Charity threatens.

What will it take for the Master Artist to heal old wounds and transform their broken marriage into a magnificent masterpiece? Could Charity's journal be enough to make Brody and Madison realize their folly and reclaim their love?

What she most needed was right there in front of her all along.

At the age of thirteen, Clarise Aylward and her two best friends each pen a wish list of things they want to achieve. Deciding to bury a tin containing their life goals, the friends vow to unearth the metal box once they've all turned forty. But as the decades pass and each girl chases her dreams, the lists are forgotten.

Heath Brock has been in love with Clarise for over twenty-seven years and counting. As a young man, he'd plucked up the courage to ask her out on a Valentine's date, but the couple succumbed to pent-up passions, sending Clarise dashing for the other side of the country.

Years after Clarise's sudden departure, Heath serves as youth pastor. He'd held out hope of Clarise's return, but buries his feelings for his childhood sweetheart when he learns she's married.

Almost penniless, divorced, and with nowhere to go, Clarise returns home to Chapel Cove, her future uncertain. She's approaching forty with her dreams in tatters. When old feelings resurface, Clarise wonders whether she's ever really fallen out of love with Heath.

What's the man of God to do when his old flame returns, seemingly to stay?

With Clarise back in town, Heath is determined not to repeat past mistakes, but if he has anything to say about it, never again will he lose the only woman he's ever loved.

The one thing he wants most in the world, she can't give him.

Her heart broken at the altar, real estate agent Julia Delpont moves south to Chapel Cove, away from the humiliation, the gossip, the stares. At least in this small town, nobody knew her story. And she had every intention of keeping it that way. No man would ever break her heart again.

After three years as an army surgeon in war-torn Afghanistan, Dr. Hudson Brock avoids the ER, choosing instead to perform scheduled surgeries at a top Dallas hospital. But neither extreme in his career has offered Hudson what he really wants—a wife and family to come home to at night. Maybe in the sleepy hollow town he'd grown up in he would find what he was looking for.

Once back in Chapel Cove, Hudson tries to find the perfect house. He suspects that finding the perfect woman will take far longer.

When Julia Delpont literally stumbles into Hudson's life, he knows he's the one who has fallen harder. But Julia is afraid to open her heart again. Especially to the handsome doctor whose deepest desires she cannot fill.

She came seeking her mother. She found so much more.

On her deathbed, Haddie Hayes's mother whispers a secret into Haddie's ear—one that she and Haddie's father had kept for twenty-eight years. The truth that Haddie wasn't born a Hayes sends this shy Kentucky girl far from the bluegrass of home to a small coastal town in Oregon in search of her birth mother. Hopefully in Chapel Cove she'll find the answers to all her questions.

EMT Riley Jordan can't help himself—he's a fixer, a helper, sometimes to his own detriment. A 911 call to Ivy's on Spruce has Riley attending to Haddie Hayes, the new girl in town. After Riley learns of Haddie's quest, he promises to help her find her birth family.

When Haddie makes the wrong assumptions, she vows to give up on her foolish crusade and go back to the only place she called home, a place she'd always felt safe and loved. But a freak accident hinders her plans of bolting from Chapel Cove.

And running from Riley…who has a secret of his own.

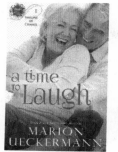

For thirty years, Brian and Elizabeth Dunham have served on the mission field. Unable to have children of their own, they've been a father and mother to countless orphans in six African countries. When an unexpected beach-house inheritance and a lung disease diagnosis coincide, they realize that perhaps God is telling them it's time to retire.

At sixty, Elizabeth is past child-bearing age. She'd long ago given up wondering whether this would be the month she would conceive. But when her best friend and neighbor jokes that Elizabeth's sudden fatigue and nausea are symptoms of pregnancy, Elizabeth finds herself walking that familiar and unwanted road again, wondering if God is pulling an Abraham and Sarah on her and Brian.

The mere notion has questions flooding Elizabeth's mind. If she were miraculously pregnant, would they have the stamina to raise a child in their golden years? Especially with Brian's health issues. And the child? Would it be healthy, or would it go through life struggling with some kind of disability? What of her own health? Could she survive giving birth?

Will what Brian and Elizabeth have dreamed of their entire married life be an old-age blessing or a curse?

Everyday life for Dr. Melanie Kerr had consisted of happy deliveries and bundles of joy...until her worst nightmare became reality. The first deaths in her OR during an emergency C-section. Both mother and child, one month before Christmas. About to perform her first Caesarean since the tragedy, Melanie loses her nerve and flees the OR. She packs her bags and catches a flight to Budapest. Perhaps time spent in the city her lost patient hailed from, can help her find the healing and peace she desperately needs to be a good doctor again.

Since the filming of Jordan's Journeys' hit TV serial "Life Begins at

Sixty" ended earlier in the year, journalist and TV host Jordan Stanson has gone from one assignment to the next. But before he can take a break, he has a final episode to film—"Zac's First Christmas". Not only is he looking forward to relaxing at his parents' seaside home, he can't wait to see his godchild, Zac, the baby born to the aging Dunhams. His boss, however, has squeezed in another documentary for him to complete before Christmas—uncovering the tragedy surrounding the doctor the country came to love on his show, the beautiful Dr. Kerr.

In order to chronicle her journey through grief and failure, Jordan has no choice but to get close to this woman. Something he has both tried and failed at in the past. He hopes through this assignment, he'll be able to help her realize the tragedy wasn't her fault. But even in a city so far away from home, work once again becomes the major catalyst to hinder romance between Jordan and Melanie.

That, and a thing called honesty.

Not every woman is fortunate enough to find her soulmate. Fewer find him twice.

JoAnn Stanson has loved and lost. Widowed a mere eighteen months ago, JoAnn is less than thrilled when her son arranges a luxury cruise around the British Isles as an early birthday gift. She's not ready to move on and "meet new people".

Caleb Blume has faced death and won. Had it not been for an unexpected Christmas present, he would surely have been pushing up daisies. Not that the silver-haired landscape architect was averse to those little flowers—he just wasn't ready to become fertilizer himself.

To celebrate his sixty-fourth birthday and the nearing two-year anniversary since he'd cheated death, Caleb books a cruise and flies to London. He is instantly drawn in a way that's never happened before to a woman he sees boarding the ship. But this woman who steals Caleb's heart is far more guarded with her own.

For JoAnn, so many little things about Caleb remind her of her late husband. It's like loving the same man twice. Yet different.

When Rafaele and Jayne meet again two years after dancing the night away together in Tuscany, is it a matter of fate or of faith?

After deciding to take a six-month sabbatical, Italian lawyer Rafaele Rossi moves from Florence back to Villa Rossi in the middle of Tuscany, resigned to managing the family farm for his aging nonna after his father's passing. Convinced a family get-together is what Nonna needs to lift her spirits, he plans an eightieth birthday party for her, making sure his siblings and cousins attend.

The Keswick jewelry store where Jayne Austin has worked for seven years closes its doors. Jayne takes her generous severance pay and heads off to Italy—Tuscany to be precise. Choosing to leave her fate in God's hands, she prays she'll miraculously bump into the handsome best man she'd danced the night away with at a friend's Tuscan wedding two years ago. She hasn't been able to forget those smoldering brown eyes and that rich Italian accent.

Jayne's prayers are answered swiftly and in the most unexpected way. Before she knows what's happening, she's a guest not only at Isabella Rossi's birthday party, but at Villa Rossi too.

When Rafaele receives what appears to be a valuable painting from an unknown benefactor, he's reminded that he doesn't want to lose Jayne again. After what he's done to drive her from the villa, though, what kind of a commitment will it take for her to stay?

She never wants to get married. He does. To her.

The day Alessandra Rossi was born, her mammà died, and a loveless life with the father who blamed the newborn for her mother's death followed. With the help of her oldest brother, Rafaele, Alessa moved away from home the moment she finished school—just like her other siblings had. Now sporting a degree in architectural history and archaeology, Alessa loves her job as a tour guide in the city of Rome—a place where she never fails to draw the attention of men. Not that Alessa cares. Fearing that the man she weds would be anything like her recently deceased father has Alessa vowing to remain single.

American missionary Michael Young has moved to Rome on a two-year mission trip. His temporary future in the country doesn't stop him from spontaneously joining Alessa's tour after spotting her outside the Colosseum. *And* being bold enough to tell her afterward that one day she'd be his wife. God had told him. And he believed Him. But Alessa shows no sign of interest in Michael.

Can anything sway the beautiful and headstrong Italian to fall in love? Can anyone convince her to put her faith and hope in the Heavenly Father, despite being raised by an earthly one who never loved her? Will her sister's prompting, or a mysterious painting, or Michael himself change Alessa's mind? About love. And about God.

Womanizer. Adulterer. Divorced. That is Lord Davis Rathbone's history. His future? He vows to never marry or fall in love again—repeating his past mistakes, not worth the risk. Then he meets Magnolia Blume, and filling his days penning poetry no longer seems an alternative to channel his pent-up feelings. With God's help, surely he can keep this rare treasure and make it work this time?

Magnolia Blume's life is perfect, except for one thing—Davis Rathbone is everything she's not looking for in a man. He doesn't strike her as one prone to the sentiments of family, or religion, but her judgments could be premature.

Magnolia must look beyond the gossip, Davis's past, and their differences to find her perfect match, because, although flawed, Davis has one redeeming quality—he is a man after God's own heart.

Rose Blume has a secret, and she's kept it for six long years. It's the reason she's convinced herself she'll have to find her joy making wedding dresses, and not wearing one.

Fashion design icon Joseph Digiavoni crosses paths with Rose for the first time since their summer romance in Florence years before, and all the old feelings for her come rushing back. Not that they ever really left. He's lived with her image since she returned to England.

Joseph and Rose are plunged into working together on the wedding outfits for the upcoming Rathbone / Blume wedding. His top client is marrying Rose's sister. But will this task prove too difficult, especially when Joseph is anxious for Rose to admit why she broke up with him in Italy and what she'd done in the months that followed?

One person holds the key to happiness for them all, if only Rose and Joseph trusted that the truth would set them free. When they finally do bare their secrets, who has the most to forgive?

Paxton Rathbone is desperate to make his way home. His inheritance long spent, he stows away on a fishing trawler bound from Norway to England only to be discovered, beaten and discarded at Scarborough's port. On home soil at last, all it would take is one phone call. But even if his mother and father are forgiving, he doubts his older brother will be.

Needing a respite from child welfare social work, Heather Blume is excited about a short-term opportunity to work at a busy North Yorkshire day center for the homeless. When one of the men she's been helping saves her from a vicious attack, she's so grateful she violates one of the most important rules in her profession—she takes him home to tend his wounds. But there's more to her actions than merely being the Good Samaritan. The man's upper-crust speech has Heather intrigued. She has no doubt he's a gentleman fallen far from grace and is determined to reunite the enigmatic young man with his family, if only he would open up about his life.

Paxton has grown too accustomed to the disdain of mankind, which perhaps is why Heather's kindness penetrates his reserves and gives him reason to hope. Reason to love? Perhaps reason to stay. But there's a fine line between love and gratitude, for both Paxton and Heather.

Holly Blume loves decorating people's homes, but that doesn't mean she's ready to play house.

Believing a house is not a home without a woman's touch, there's nothing more Reverend Christopher Stewart would like than to find a wife. What woman would consider him marriage material, though, with an aging widowed father to look after, especially one who suffers from Alzheimer's?

When Christopher arrives at his new parish, he discovers the church ladies have arranged a welcome surprise—an office makeover by congregant and interior designer Holly Blume. Impressed with Miss Blume's work, Christopher decides to contract the talented lady to turn the rectory into a home. When they begin to clash more than their taste in color, will the revamp come to the same abrupt end as his only romantic relationship?

Despite their differences, Holly resolves to finish the job of redesigning the Stewart home, while Christopher determines to re-form Holly's heart.

Top London chef Clover Blume has one chance to become better acquainted with Jonathan Spalding away from the mayhem of her busy restaurant where he frequently dines—usually with a gorgeous woman at her side. When the groomsman who is supposed to escort her at her sister's New Year's Eve wedding is delayed because of business, Clover begins to wonder whether she really wants to waste time with a player whose main focus in life is making money rather than keeping promises.

Jonathan lives the good life. There's one thing, however, the London Investment Banker's money hasn't managed to buy: a woman to love—one worthy of his mother's approval. Is it possible though, that the auburn-haired beauty who is to partner with him at his best friend's wedding—a wedding he stands to miss thanks to a glitch in a deal worth millions—is finding a way into his heart?

But what will it cost Jonathan to realize it profits him nothing to gain the world, yet lose his soul?

And the girl.

Who am I? The question has Taylor Cassidy journeying from one side of America to the other seeking an answer. Almost five years brings her no closer to the truth. Now an award-winning photojournalist for Wines & Vines, Taylor is sent on assignment to South Africa to discover the inspiration behind Aimee Amour, the DeBois estate's flagship wine. Mystery has enshrouded the story of the woman for whom the wine is named.

South African winegrower Armand DeBois's world is shattered when a car accident leaves him in a coma for three weeks, and his young wife dead. The road of recovery and mourning is dark, and Armand teeters between falling away from God and falling into His comforting arms.

When Armand and Taylor meet, questions arise for them both. While the country and the winegrower hold a strange attraction for Taylor, Armand struggles with the uncertainty of whether he's falling in love with his past or his future.

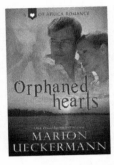

When his wife dies in childbirth, conservationist Simon Hartley pours his life into raising his daughter and his orphan elephants. He has no time, or desire, to fall in love again. Or so he thinks.

Wanting to escape English society and postpone an arranged marriage, Lady Abigail Chadwick heads to Africa for a year to teach the children of the Good Shepherd Orphanage. Upon her arrival she is left stranded at Livingstone airport...until a reluctant Simon comes to her rescue.

Now only fears born of his loss, and secrets of the life she's tried to leave behind, can stonewall their romance, budding in the heart of Africa.

Escaping his dangerous past, former British rock star Justin "The Phoenix" Taylor flees as far away from home as possible to Australia. A marked man with nothing left but his guitar and his talent, Justin is desperate to start over yet still live off the grid. Loneliness and the need to feel a connection to the London pastor who'd saved his life draw Justin to Ella's Barista Art Coffee Shop—the famous and trendy Melbourne establishment belonging to Pastor Jim Anderson's niece.

Intrigued by the bearded stranger who looks vaguely familiar, Ella Anderson wearies of serving him his regular flat white espresso every morning with no more than a greeting for conversation. Ella decides to discover his secrets, even if it requires coaxing him with her elaborate latte art creations. And muffins.

Justin gradually begins to open up to Ella but fears his past will collide with their future. When it does, Ella must decide whether they have a future at all.

1972. Every day in Belfast, Northern Ireland, holds risk, especially for the mayor's daughter. But Dr. Olivia O'Hare has a heart for people and chooses to work on the wrong side of a city where colors constantly clash. The orange and green of the Republicans pitted against the red and blue of those loyal to Britain. While they might share the common hue of white, it brings no peace.

Caught between the Republicans and Loyalists' conflict, blue-collar worker Ryann Doyle has to wonder if there's life before death. The answer seems to be a resounding, 'No'. His mother is dead, his father's a drunk, and his younger brother, Declan, is steeped in the Provisional IRA. Then he crosses paths with Olivia O'Hare.

After working four days straight, mopping up PIRA's latest act of terror, Olivia is exhausted. All she wants is to go home and rest. But when she drives away from Royal Victoria Hospital, rest is the last thing Olivia gets.

When Declan kidnaps the Lord Mayor of Belfast's daughter, Ryann has to find a way to rescue the dark-haired beauty, though it means he must turn his back on his own flesh and blood for someone he just met.

While Ginger Murphy completes her music studies, childhood sweetheart and neighbor, Brad O'Sullivan betrays her with the new girl next door. Heartbroken, Ginger escapes as far away as she can go—to Australia—for five long years. During this time, Brad's shotgun marriage fails. Besides his little boy, Jamie, one other thing in his life has turned out sweet and successful—his pastry business.

When her mother's diagnosed with heart failure, Ginger has no choice but to return to the green grass of Ireland. As a sought-after wedding flautist, she quickly establishes herself on home soil. Although she loves her profession, she fears she'll never be more than the entertainment at these joyous occasions. And that she's doomed to bump into the wedding cake chef she tries to avoid. Brad broke her heart once. She won't give him a chance to do it again.

A gingerbread house contest at church to raise funds for the homeless has Ginger competing with Brad. Both are determined to win—Ginger the contest, Brad her heart. But when a dear old saint challenges that the Good Book says the first shall be last, and the last first, Ginger has to decide whether to back down from contending with Brad and embrace the true meaning of Christmas—peace on earth, good will to all men. Even the Irishman she'd love to hate.

Writer's block and a looming Christmas novel deadline have romance novelist, Sarah Jones, heading for the other side of the world on a whim.

Niklas Toivonen offers cozy Lapland accommodation, but when his aging father falls ill, Niklas is called upon to step into his father's work clothes to make children happy. Red is quite his color.

Fresh off the airplane, a visit to Santa sets Sarah's muse into overdrive. The man in red is not only entertaining, he's young—with gorgeous blue eyes. Much like her new landlord's, she discovers. Santa and Niklas quickly become objects of research—for her novel, and her curiosity.

Though she's written countless happily-ever-afters, Sarah doubts she'll ever enjoy her own. Niklas must find a way to show her how to leave the pain of her past behind, so she can find love and faith once more.

Opera singer, Skye Hunter, returns to the land of her birth as leading lady in Phantom of the Opera. This is her first trip back to bonnie Scotland since her mother whisked her away to Australia after Skye's father died sixteen years ago.

When Skye decides to have dinner at McGuire's, she's not going there only for Mary McGuire's shepherd's pie. Her first and only love, Callum McGuire, still plays his guitar and sings at the family-owned tavern.

Callum has never stopped loving Skye. Desperate to know if she's changed under her mother's influence, he keeps his real profession hidden. Would she want him if he was still a singer in a pub? But when Skye's worst nightmare comes true, Callum reveals his secret to save the woman he loves.

Can Skye and Callum rekindle what they lost, or will her mother threaten their future together once again?

"If women were meant to fly, the skies would be pink."

Those were the first words Anjelica Joergensen heard from renowned wingsuiter, Kyle Sheppard, when they joined an international team in Oslo to break the formation flying Guinness World Record. This wouldn't be the last blunder Kyle would make around the beautiful Norwegian.

The more Anjelica tries to avoid Kyle, the more the universe pushes them together. Despite their awkward start, she finds herself reluctantly attracted to the handsome New Zealander. But beneath his saintly exterior, is Kyle just another daredevil looking for the next big thrill?

Falling for another wingsuiter would only be another love doomed.

When a childhood sweetheart comes between them, Kyle makes a foolish agreement which jeopardizes the event and endangers his life, forcing Angelica to make a hard choice.

Is she the one who'll clip his wings?

Can he be the wind beneath hers?

Three weeks alone at a friend's summer cottage on a Finnish lake to fast and pray. That was Adam Carter's plan. But sometimes plans go awry.

On an impromptu trip to her family's secluded summer cottage, the last thing Eveliina Mikkola expected to find was a missionary from the other side of the world—in her sauna.

Determined to stay, Eveliina will do whatever it takes—from shortcrust pastry to shorts—to send the man of God packing. This island's too small for them both.

Adam Carter, however, is not about to leave.

Will he be able to resist her temptations?

Can she withstand his prayers?

Their outdoor wedding planned for the middle of Africa's rainy summer, chances are it'll pour on Mirabelle Kelly's bridal parade—after all, she is marrying Noah Raines.

To make matters worse, the African Rain Queen, Modjadji, is invited to the wedding.

Mirabelle must shun her superstitions and place her faith in the One who really controls the weather.

Note: This short story is in the *Dancing up a Storm* anthology.

Made in the USA
Columbia, SC
01 April 2024

33869296R00102